PRAISE FOR *TWITCH*

"A winged masterpiece."
MAZ EVANS

"Enthralling from beginning to end, it really touched
my young bird-loving heart! Just wonderful!"
DARA MCANULTY

"Birds, mystery and fowl play! What more could you want?"
GILL LEWIS

"Glorious! Full of excitement and wonder!"
SOPHIE ANDERSON

"Cracking characters, beyond pacy plotting and
an ending that is almost Bugsy Malone-esque!"
PHIL EARLE

"*Twitch* is a compelling read – an adventure mystery
with birds – what more could any reader want?"
STEPHEN MOSS

"Adventure, friendship and the pure unassuming beauty
of nature … a book that could have been a collaboration
between David Attenborough and Roald Dahl."
DR JESS FRENCH

"A superb adventure of friendship, bravery
and the wonderful world of birds."
THE BOOKSELLER

TWITCH

WALKER BOOKS

M. G. LEONARD

WALKER
BOOKS

First published 2021 by Walker Books Ltd
87 Vauxhall Walk, London SE11 5HJ

2 4 6 8 10 9 7 5 3 1

Text © 2021 MG Leonard Ltd.
Cover illustrations © 2021 Paddy Donnelly
Map illustration © 2021 Laurissa Jones

Printed and bound by CPI Group (UK) Ltd, Croydon CR0 4YY

British Library Cataloguing in Publication Data:
a catalogue record for this book is available from the British Library

ISBN 978-1-4063-8937-1

www.walker.co.uk

MIX
Paper from
responsible sources
FSC
www.fsc.org
FSC® C020471

In loving memory of
Jane Sparling,
1948–2020

"I hope you love birds too. It is economical.
It saves going to heaven."

— **Emily Dickinson**

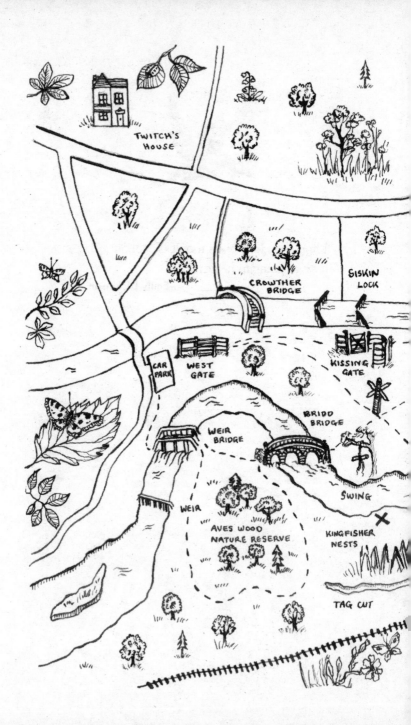

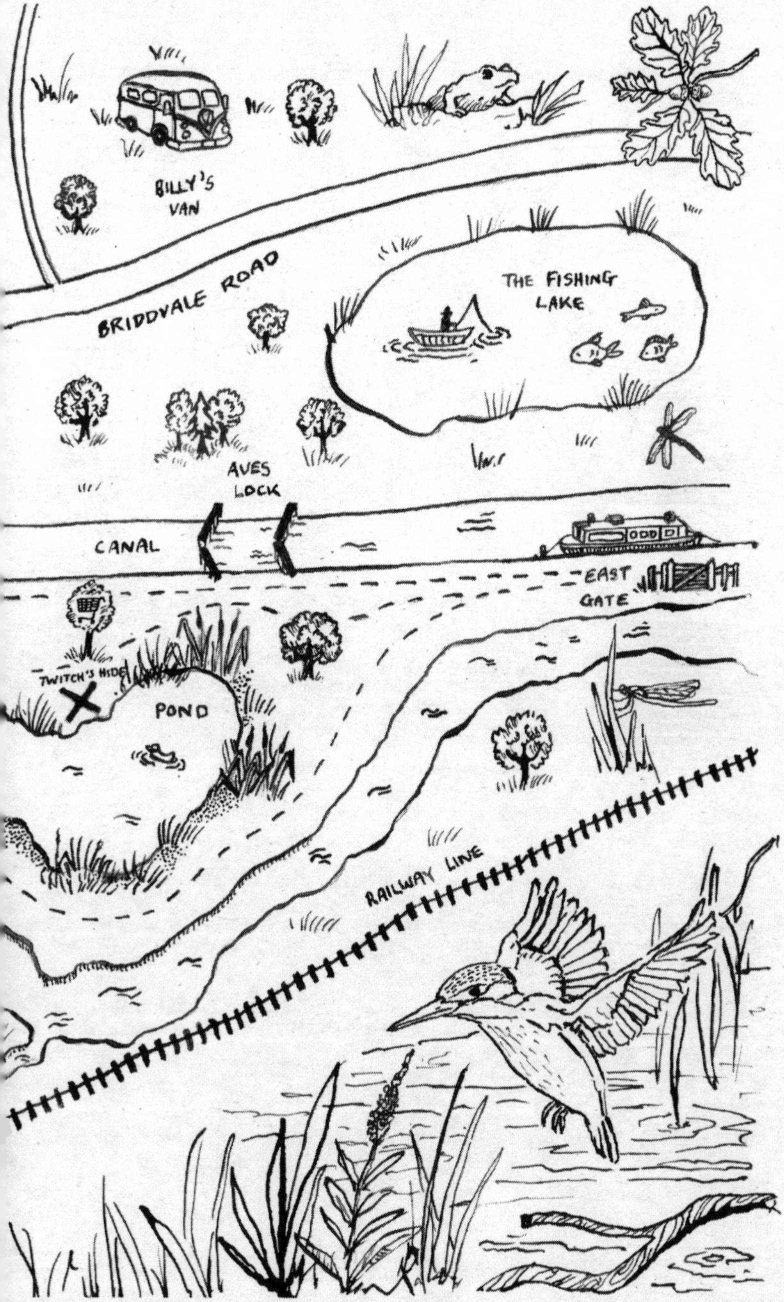

BILLY'S VAN

BRIDDVALE ROAD

THE FISHING LAKE

AVES LOCK

CANAL

EAST GATE

TWITCH'S HIDE

POND

RAILWAY LINE

1

ROCK DOVE

"*Kill it!*"

Twitch stopped dead on the path to the main school building, ignoring the spots of rain landing on his cheeks. He listened.

"Go on. *Do it!*"

The feverish voice belonged to Jack Cappleman, a charismatic boy with caramel-coloured hair who'd moved to Briddvale a few months ago. From the moment he'd sloped into school with his city boy manner, everyone had danced to Jack's tune, following him like the Pied Piper's rats.

"My dad says if you crush a pigeon its eyes'll pop out," said a deep voice that could only belong to Vernon Boon. Vernon was the size of a grown-up and as sensitive as a sandbag. Outside school he always wore wellies, and his dad ran the local abattoir. Vernon rarely spoke to Twitch, although he shoved him on a daily basis, laughing if he stumbled or fell.

Twitch heard a chorus of *"Ewww!"*, *"Let's see!"*, *"Do it!"* and *"I can't look!"*

Bending down, he picked up a flint from the barren flower bed that ran alongside the chemistry block and slipped the stone into his blazer pocket, hurrying to the corner of the building. Peering round at where the big silver dustbins were kept, he saw four boys crowded around something on the ground.

Terry Vallis, a skinny boy with dark curly hair and braces, was babbling. "Are you sure this is a good idea? I mean, it's the eye-popping thing. It's making me feel sick. I'm not going to puke or anything, but..."

Jack started to chant. *"Do it! Do it! Do it!"*

"Do what?" Twitch asked loudly.

The boys were startled by his voice.

"Ozuru, you're supposed to be keeping watch!" Jack scolded the short boy standing at the edge of the group.

Ozuru Sawa shrugged and looked away.

"Ooorrrhh! Ooorrrhh!"

Twitch recognized the alarmed calls of a bird, saw the brick Vernon clutched in his fist, and folded his arms to try to contain the anger that blazed in his chest. "You're going to kill a rock dove?"

"No." Vernon sniffed. "Gonna kill a pigeon."

"A pigeon is descended from a rock dove." Twitch glared at the boys through his brackish-blond fringe. He was a bit taller than Ozuru and stronger than Terry, but the odds of him surviving a punch-up with either Jack or Vernon were slim, and he had no chance against all four of them. "That bird has as much right to live as you do."

"It's vermin." A mean smile twisted Jack's face and he stepped forward. "We're performing a public service by exterminating it."

"It isn't." Twitch's forehead throbbed as Vernon's fist tightened around his brick and the terrified bird kept calling. He blinked furiously, trying to calm down.

"Are you going to stop us?" Jack made a show of looking past Twitch. "On *your own*?" The three boys gathered behind Jack, who was blinking theatrically, mimicking Twitch's nervous habit. "Tell me, birdbrain, what's it like being such a loser that your only friends have feathers?"

"Yeah, feathers, heh-heh," the others echoed.

Jack called out to the pigeon. "Hey, birdie, don't worry, your best bud is here to save you." He mimed counting the boys. "Oh, wait. There's only one of him and four of us." He pulled a mock sad face and the other boys laughed. Jack grabbed the brick from Vernon, raising it as if to strike the bird.

"NO!" Twitch lurched forward, driving his hand into his pocket, grasping the flint and hurling it hard. The stone sailed through the air, hitting Jack on the side of the head.

Jack cried out, dropping the brick and clutching his hand to his temple. The brick landed on Vernon's foot. He roared, hopping about as Twitch ran head first into Terry's stomach. Terry fell over with a yelp. Twitch felt Vernon grab him around the middle and whirl him away. He saw Ozuru staring at him with a stunned look on his face.

"I'm bleeding!" Jack cried, staring at a red smudge on his hand.

Twitch felt a flash of satisfaction, but it was cut short by Vernon throwing him backwards. He slammed into the bins. As he hit the ground, all the air was walloped out of his lungs. His eyes snapped wide as he desperately tried, and failed, to breathe in. He felt the fire of a kick to his ribs and saw Ozuru standing over him.

"I'm going to need stitches," Jack cursed as a trickle of blood ran down the side of his face.

"I think my toe's broken," Vernon remarked, apparently unbothered.

"You'll regret this, Twitch!" Jack barked, marching away, shouting over his shoulder, "This isn't over!"

"This isn't over," Ozuru repeated as he helped Terry to his feet. He was bent double with his arms wrapped around his stomach.

As Ozuru and Terry stumbled after Jack, Vernon grinned and Twitch flinched, thinking he was going to punch him, but instead he snorted and lumbered after the others.

Twitch lay still, waiting for his breath to return. His ribs were sore, but it was nothing he hadn't felt a hundred times. The main thing was the bird was alive. Getting to his knees, he crawled towards the panicked cooing. Tucking his fringe behind his ear, he saw an unhappy rock dove trapped between the brick wall of the chemistry lab and the side of a silver bin.

The pigeon's head jerked back, emerald bib shimmering, its orange eyes staring out of the puffed-up ball of storm-cloud grey. The bird had one healthy foot, but the other leg ended in a lump of gristle, and one of its ashen wings was injured, feathers ragged.

"What did they do to you, eh?" Twitch whispered as a tremor of emotion shook his body. "You're scared half to death." He slid off his rucksack and blazer, pulling his jumper off over his head and laying it on his knees. He inched towards the bird. Then, in a swift move, he tenderly cupped his hands around it, lifting it onto the jumper. "There you go," he cooed as he pulled up the sides of the sweater to make a dark cocoon for the frightened pigeon.

Rising to his feet, Twitch cradled the bundle of bird with one arm. He peered over the top of the open bin. There was a stack of flattened cardboard boxes inside. He took one and put it on the ground, folding in the flaps and building the box with his spare hand. Then he lowered his bundle into it, peeling back the jumper.

Lunchtime was nearly over, but Twitch couldn't leave the bird behind the chemistry block. Jack and his gang would be back, and this time they would kill it. If he took the bird home, he'd never get back in time for afternoon registration. He wondered if there was anywhere in the school that he could hide it until the end of the day, but couldn't think of anywhere.

"You're not safe here," he said to the distressed bird.

"Bcrrooo-bcrrooo," the pigeon replied.

Twitch stuffed his blazer into his rucksack, no longer aware of his bruised ribs or the falling rain. He knew he'd be in trouble, but some things were more important than double PE. Picking up the box carefully, he walked out of the school gates and headed for home.

2

WORMS FOR FOOD

Three months had passed since Twitch had saved the injured pigeon. Walking out of school with the bird in the box had cost him a week of detentions. He'd made an enemy of Jack Cappleman and become more of a social outcast than he already was, but it had been worth it.

Twitch had named the pigeon Scabby, on account of his numerous grisly injuries, and built him a pigeon loft from a tall thin wardrobe he'd found at the dump. The pigeon's wounds healed and he was happy to hang around as long as he was being given free food and shelter. To Twitch's delight a female pigeon took a shine to him and they began courting, eventually building a nest in the loft. She was a pretty bird with a slender white neck and dark eyes set in a charcoal face. He called her Maude, after his grandmother.

Within a week of Maude moving in with Scabby, their nest boasted two eggs.

From Scabby and Maude's eggs hatched Squeaker and Frazzle, two chicks that began life dodo-shaped and pink with a fine yellow down. Twitch had watched with amazement as, over ten days, they grew bigger, darker and stronger. Now, more than a month after they'd hatched, the squabs looked pigeon-shaped.

Today was the last day of school before the summer holidays and the sun shone white-hot. The tarmac under Twitch's feet felt sticky as he hurried out of the school gates, the deep green of the distant hills calling to him. The air was charged with the electricity of freedom. The summer holidays rolled out before him like a magic carpet of perfect possibilities. No school, no homework, and pigeons to train.

"Oi, Twitch. *DUCK!*"

Something hit his back. Twitch looked round to see what it was. On the ground was a silver takeaway container; beside it lay scattered bones and charred flakes of brown skin. Peals of laughter instinctively made Twitch drop his chin to his chest, letting his hair cover his face. He picked up his pace, jamming his hands into his pockets, his shoulders rising to his ears, knowing if he ran, they would chase him.

"You hungry, Twitch?" someone shouted. "Wanna eat a friend?"

Another silver container hit his leg and bones flew.

A girl, her name was Pamela Hardacre, made quacking noises, and then they all joined in. A mean choir of ducks, honking and hooting at him.

"Duck! Get it?" Jack called out. "It's duck, Twitch, so you'd better *DUCK*!"

Another silver missile hit the back of Twitch's head. He felt the scratch of crumbs slipping down the collar of his school shirt and shivered.

"Yeah, I get it," he called out, putting one foot in front of the other, telling himself that each step took him closer to home.

"Then why aren't you laughing?" There was a hint of menace in Jack's voice. "It's a joke! Where's your sense of humour?"

"Leave me alone," Twitch replied wearily. But he knew Jack wasn't going to let him walk away from year seven without punishing him one last time for the pink scar above his cheekbone.

"Aw, is *Corvus* sad?" Jack taunted. "Does the dead birdie make him want to cry?"

There were murmurs and titters as other children caught the scent of blood. A crowd was building.

It was jarring to hear Jack use his real name. People only did that when he was in trouble. "Twitch" was a nickname he'd earned because he had a nervous habit of blinking, but he'd always liked the name because his grandad had told him a twitcher was a birdwatcher with an interest in rare birds. Everyone called him Twitch; he even thought of himself as Twitch.

Someone grabbed his rucksack and yanked him backwards.

Jack stepped in front of him. "You should thank me."

"What for?"

"For bringing you a snack." Jack held the remains of a duck leg in his right hand. He threw his left arm around Twitch's neck, grabbing him in a headlock. "Eat it," he growled, thrusting the leg in Twitch's face.

Twitch turned his head away, struggling. "I'm vegetarian."

Jack pushed the scaly duck leg against Twitch's lips. *"Eat it!"*

"Get off," Twitch muttered through clenched teeth. The smell of the meat was making his stomach turn. He didn't want it near his mouth. "I'll puke!"

Jack let go as Twitch retched.

Someone swiped at his feet and Twitch fell to the ground. He rolled away, ending up on the grass verge beside the pavement, trapped between Jack and the peeling silver trunk of a birch tree.

"Aw, Twitch loves the birdies too much to eat them." Jack stood over him, sneering.

"If he loves birds so much," Pamela's mocking voice called out, "why doesn't he eat what they eat?"

"Yeah!" Jack's face lit up. *"Worms!"* He glanced over his shoulder at the watching faces. "Find me a worm. Twitch is hungry."

Twitch tried to get up, but Jack put a foot on his chest. "Oh no. You're not going anywhere."

Vernon kneeled, pulling a wooden ruler from his bag, and started digging in the turf. Terry dropped to his knees beside him.

"Found one!" Vernon said, yanking a wriggling pink spaghetti string from its cool dark hiding place.

"Yummy yummy," Jack said, holding out his hand for the worm. "Open your mouth, Twitch, there's a good baby bird."

Vernon handed the worm to Jack. Everyone leaned in to see if Twitch would be made to eat it. A girl called Tara Dabiri, who was stood beside Pamela, went pale. "I can't watch," she murmured, her hand over her mouth. "This is cruel."

"To the worm," Pamela laughed.

With his free hand Jack grabbed Twitch's chin and tried to prise his mouth open. Twitch shook his head from side to side.

"Vernon, hold him," Jack instructed, and Twitch felt hands lock his head into position. "Terry, sit on his legs." Jack smiled, pinching Twitch's nose and dangling the worm over his tightly closed mouth. "You're going to eat this worm, birdbrain."

"*HEY!*" a man's voice rang out. "What's going on?"

And like a flock of startled starlings the children scattered.

By the time Twitch had sat up, Jack, Vernon, Terry and the others were pelting away up the road. A man wearing a white tee under an open blue chequered shirt and a black leather trilby sauntered over. His knowing smile was framed by a close beard and his blue eyes twinkled. A chunky gold bracelet slid over his wrist as he reached down to help Twitch to his feet. "You all right, kid?"

Twitch nodded.

"They friends of yours?" The man had a lilt to his voice, which made Twitch think he was Scottish or Irish.

Twitch shook his head.

"Enemies?"

Twitch shrugged.

"Yeah, I got picked on at school too." The man gave Twitch a sympathetic look. "Why the worm?"

The man was definitely Irish. Twitch heard his mum's voice telling him not to talk to strangers. But she'd never said what to do if the stranger had saved you from having to eat a worm. He figured he should be polite.

"I like birds. I keep them."

"Really?" The man looked surprised. "What kind?"

"Pigeons, and chickens, but others nest in my garden." Twitch could feel himself blinking. He was uncomfortable talking about himself to grown-ups. "Right now, we've got a pair of blue tits in our nesting box and the swallows come back every year."

"Really? My favourite bird is the swift," the man said, looking interested.

"The scythe-winged flight sleeper," Twitch said, then blushed. "That's what I call them. Swifts. They can sleep and fly at the same time."

"That's the one. Lovely little birds." The man gave him a look, as if the two of them understood something few people did. He made an exploding gesture with his hand. "They blow my mind."

Twitch grinned.

"I'm just passing through Briddvale, I thought I

might do a bit of birdwatching whilst I'm here. Are there any good spots you'd recommend? A wood, or that sort of a thing?"

"Oh, yes." Twitch was thrilled that his saviour was a fellow birdwatcher. "You should go to the nature reserve. It's called Aves Wood. It's got a mix of habitat and a big patch of wetland. It's part of a green corridor."

"A green corridor?"

"Yeah, you know, a route for migrating birds. There's always a chance of seeing something good at Aves Wood. There are woodpeckers, bullfinches and kingfishers too."

"Great. That's great, kid. Aves Wood. I'll check it out." The man looked over his shoulder as the sound of approaching police sirens interrupted his train of thought. "Hey, a newsagent's." He pointed. "I need a paper. How about I get you something sweet to take away the flavour of worm, in exchange for a few local tips?" He extended his hand. "My name's Billy, by the way."

"I'm Twitch." He awkwardly shook Billy's hand as they crossed the road. "You don't have to get me anything. I didn't eat the worm."

Billy pushed the newsagent's door open for him. "In you go, Twitch. Unusual name that. Grab yourself a chocolate bar, on me. Sugar is good for a shock."

"Wasn't a shock," Twitch replied. "They do it all the time."

"Even more of a reason." Billy pointed at the rack of sweets.

Mr Bettany, the newsagent, smiled at Twitch. The kindly man who wore a flat cap, indoors and out, employed him on Saturdays to do a paper round.

Staring at the brightly coloured sweet wrappers, Twitch was torn between temptation and guilt. His mum would be cross if she found out he'd accepted sweets from a stranger. But, if he took them to his hide in the woods and ate them there, she wouldn't need to know. And Billy seemed nice. He was a birder, like Twitch. Twitch missed having someone to talk to about birds. His grandad had taken him birdwatching when he was little, but since he'd passed away Twitch's expeditions had all been solo.

He selected a packet of Fruit Gums because they wouldn't melt and put them on the counter beside Billy's newspaper. He glanced at the headline *Robber Ryan on the Rampage!* Below it was a picture of a person with a shaved head. Billy paid Mr Bettany, whilst chatting amiably about the weather and the state of the roads.

"See you tomorrow, Twitch." Mr Bettany waved as they left.

Outside, Twitch thanked Billy for rescuing him from Jack and for the Fruit Gums.

"You going to be OK getting home?"

Twitch's heart jumped; he knew he should be guarded about where he lived. "I'll go home the back way. Mum'll be looking out for me," he lied, glancing at Billy between blinks. He wasn't going home, but he wasn't about to admit that to a stranger.

"Smart thinking," Billy tapped his head. "Listen, I'm going to check out this Aves Wood – maybe take a few walks, look at the birds. I'm travelling in my camper van. I was wondering, is there somewhere near by, out of the way, that I could park? You know" – he leaned down and said out of the side of his mouth – "somewhere I won't have to pay."

"There's the bottom field of Patchem's farm, off Briddvale Road," Twitch replied, frowning at this furtive request. "He lets people park there sometimes."

"Patchem's farm. Cheers, that's very helpful." Billy winked conspiratorially. "See you around, Twitch. Mind you stay away from those worms." He chuckled, lifted his hand in farewell and sauntered off down the road.

Twitch stared at Billy's back, watching him go. He felt a flash of guilt for being suspicious of the man, then grinned at the packet of Fruit Gums. The school holidays hadn't got off to a bad start. He turned, going in the opposite direction to Billy, heading straight for his secret hide in Aves Wood.

3

AVES WOOD

The Aves Wood Nature Reserve was built on an old fly-tipping site. Rare plants grew there because fly ash from the coal mines had made the soil alkaline. And, despite the name, not all of it was woodland. Some of it was meadow and a large part of it was wetland. It was a city for insects, a fine dining experience for birds, and Twitch's favourite place in the whole world. You never knew what bird might visit the banks of the River Bridd or choose to nest around the pond in the boggy swamp of the wetland.

Twitch entered Aves Wood through a kissing gate beside the canal, which ran almost parallel to the river. Immediately stepping off the footpath, he glanced about, checking no one had seen him, then dashed through the undergrowth, making his way towards the pond, inhaling the heady scent of pine resin and smiling to himself as he trod carefully over tree roots and badger setts, trying not to leave footprints that might lead anyone to his hide.

As the ground became mushy and sodden, the trees thinned, and he saw the pond stretching out in front of him, its surface shimmering like a mirage in the heat. He heard the mouse-like squeak of an oystercatcher and scanned the reeds for the black and white wader with the long orange beak. But the barking of dogs broke his concentration and he dropped into a squat. Peering through a tangle of brambles, he saw two police officers being tugged along by a pair of excited Alsatians on leads. They were ten or eleven metres away, off the footpath. Twitch was surprised. It was unusual to see the police in Aves Wood, and he'd never seen them with dogs. He sniffed the air, wondering if some of the college kids had started a fire, but detected no smoke, just the comforting earthy fragrance of the woods.

Circumnavigating the pond, wary of the deep pools of water around the bulrushes that masqueraded as solid ground, Twitch picked his way across a clearing towards a thicket of trees, relaxing now he knew he was hidden from the public paths by dense foliage and distance.

A bone-shakingly loud *fffddd-fffddd-fffddd* drew his eyes to the sky as a police helicopter flew over, surprisingly low. Alarmed birds, flushed from their nests in the tussocks around the water's edge, called out in distress. Feeling exposed, Twitch sprinted, ducking as he pushed his way into the shadowy copse, ignoring the scratch of whip-thin branches. He glanced about nervously, his pulse galloping and his breath short. What were the police looking for? It was a shock to see people here. It was a secluded part of the reserve because of the dangers of the waterlogged land. He stood stock-still, watching the helicopter pass, waiting for the peaceful chirps and buzz of the woods to return.

Reaching down into a green mass of unfurling fronds, Twitch released a coat hanger that was attached to a thin rope looping up into a tree. As he pulled it, a flap of ferns lifted, revealing an opening low to the ground. Hooking the hanger over a branch, he dropped to all fours and crawled inside his hide.

To the left of the door was the watching window – a wide rectangular panel that could be propped open for birdwatching. Twitch opened it and peered out. On the far side of the pond he saw three sailing boats and officers in uniform aboard, wearing life jackets, poking about in the reeds with long sticks. He thought about the headline on Billy's newspaper.

Sliding his rucksack off, Twitch sat down on a blue plastic milk crate that served as a chair or a table and waited for his eyes to adjust to the shadows. In the middle of the floor, directly below the apex of the tepee, was a fire pit encircled with flints. One of the roof sections between the apex and the tree branch lifted up and flipped over, making a hole to let smoke out. But Twitch hadn't yet dare light a fire, for fear it might attract attention.

In the beginning, Twitch's hide was just a tepee of sticks, built against an ancient beech that grew in a ring of coppiced hazel trees whose roots had woven together to make firm ground. He'd constructed it to watch the wetland birds. Last summer, the tepee had expanded into a wild fort as Twitch's building plans grew more and more ambitious. Beyond the tepee room was a second space that he'd made watertight, so he might camp out here some night. It was the shape and size of a triangular two-man tent and constructed from a sheet of plastic thrown over a bough of the beech tree. It was walled in with branches, wedged into trenches in the ground and tied where they criss-crossed at the top. He'd filled the trenches with soil, banking it up to keep out rivulets of rain. Gaps were stuffed with leafy sticks and he'd woven fern fronds through them, plugging any holes with moss, until the hide had blended in with the forest on all sides. Unfortunately, the plants Twitch had used to camouflage his den had turned brown and crumbled. So, at the end of last summer, he'd brought his spade to Aves Wood and dug up ferns, teasels, thistles, nettles and brambles, replanting them around the hide. In the spring, as the brambles shot tendrils along the forest floor, he'd woven them into the external walls. The teasels shot up, the thistles fanned out, the nettles multiplied. Together they created a line of defence, spiky foot soldiers that kept away the curious with their arsenal of thorns and stings.

Everything appeared to be as he'd left it last Sunday. Sweeping his hands across the earth floor, he moved a layer of dirt, exposing the top of a buried storage box. He popped off the lid. Inside was his birdwatching kit and an assortment of useful objects, including a red tartan cushion, dry kindling, an umbrella, a torch, a pair of gardening gloves and a box of matches in a sealed sandwich bag. He put the Fruit Gums from Billy into the box and lifted out his most prized possession: the battered leather case that held his grandad's binoculars. The heavy spyglasses evoked memories of quiet hours sat beside the kind old man he thought of as his dad, being taught the names of plants whilst learning to be patient. "Patience," his grandad always used to say, "is the silent call that brings the owls, the hawks and the falcons."

Twitch hung the binoculars around his neck and crawled into the triangular room. Going to the back wall, he slid aside a stumpy branch, as if shooting a bolt, revealing a hole the perfect size for his spyglasses. He slotted the binoculars into the gap and moved the dial between the lenses until the distant footpath came into focus. Something was happening in Aves Wood and he wanted to know what it was.

His view was patchy, obscured by tree trunks and thorny scrub, but there were three sections of the footpath that he could see clearly. He waited, calm and patient, and was rewarded by the sight of a woman in a suit, followed by a troop of officers in uniform. She was pointing, giving orders. The troop divided and dispersed.

Twitch felt a lurch of alarm. The police were searching for someone or something in Aves Wood. What if they came here, and discovered his hide? The summer would be ruined! He had made plans. Tomorrow he was going to begin training his squabs, Squeaker and Frazzle.

He planned to take them out on their maiden homing flight, then spend the rest of the day here, watching the wetland birds, updating his field journal and making improvements to his hide.

A flash of yellow caught his eye and he retrained his binoculars. He blinked, surprised to see two girls hiding in the undergrowth, peering over a fallen tree trunk at the footpath. The elder one had a waterfall of tight dark curls down her back and brooding elfin features. She was wearing jeans, a rainbow T-shirt, and carrying a plastic bag. The other girl, who looked a few years younger, had honey-brown curly hair scraped into a puffball ponytail on top of her head. She was wearing shorts with a yellow net skirt over the top and a pink vest under a powder-blue criss-cross cardigan. She looked frightened, huddled up against the older girl. The two girls were alike enough for Twitch to guess they were sisters. He couldn't hear what they were saying, but he could tell the older girl was reassuring the younger. Their expressions were serious, and their gestures were animated.

Could the police be after them?

There were too many people stomping about Aves Wood to watch birds, and Twitch was curious to know what was going on. Why were so many police officers, dogs and a helicopter in the nature reserve? Keeping his binoculars around his neck, he covered the storage box, sweeping the dirt back over it to keep it hidden. Pulling on his rucksack, Twitch left the hide, making sure it was secure. He decided to make his way round to the rabbit track that wove a thin path through the nettles towards the girls' hiding place and see if he could find out what they were up to.

4

A SILVER KINGFISHER

By the time Twitch reached the end of the rabbit track, the girls had gone. He felt deflated. Now he'd never know why they were hiding or looking scared. He didn't think they were local. He'd never seen them before and Briddvale was a small town. Most likely they were early summer tourists.

Going over to the fallen tree trunk, Twitch crouched in the same spot the girls had, and peered over the top. He had a clear view of the main footpath. At the distant crossroads stood a squadron of police officers with stern faces. Whatever was happening in Aves Wood, Twitch realized with a thrill that he shouldn't be here.

He crawled backwards, and his eye glimpsed the shimmer of a violet ground beetle scurrying under leaf mulch, hunting for slugs to eat. It scuttled over a string of blue and green beads, half hidden in the leaves. He picked it up between thumb and forefinger. It was a bracelet with a tiny silver bird dangling from it: a kingfisher. It felt like a sign. He slipped it into his pocket. If he saw the girls again, he'd use the bracelet as an excuse to talk to them and find out why they'd been spying on the police.

Thinking it best not to look suspicious, Twitch marched upright and noisily through the trees to the main footpath; and, sure enough, before he got there an officer had called out to him.

"You, young man, come here."

"Yes, sir," Twitch obeyed. "What's going on, Officer?" he asked. "Why are there so many police here?"

"We're combing the woods," the officer replied. "Are you on your own?"

Twitch nodded.

"Birdwatching?" He pointed at the binoculars around Twitch's neck and smiled.

Twitch nodded again.

"Seen anyone around here that you don't know?"

Twitch thought of the two girls but was already shaking his head. The girls had looked scared of the police and he didn't want to get them into trouble.

"OK, well, I need you to exit that way and go

straight home." He pointed in the opposite direction to the way Twitch needed to go. "We're clearing the reserve."

"Yes, Officer." Twitch turned, then paused. "Is it a bad crime? I mean no one's been murdered, have they?"

"Nothing like that," the officer reassured him. "Yesterday, a dangerous prisoner escaped from Dovelock Prison. They've been spotted in the area, and we've reason to believe they are coming here."

"Why?"

"To collect something," the officer said with meaning.

"Is it Robber Ryan?" Twitch asked, recalling the name in the headline.

"I'm not at liberty to say," the officer said, nodding. "Now, please, go home. And tell your parents they should lock all the doors and windows tonight. All right? Off you go."

Twitch hurried away down the path. Robber Ryan was in Briddvale! He pictured a tall figure dressed like a highwayman with a black mask and carrying a pistol. The thought of a gun made him pick up his pace. Exiting the reserve through the east gate meant going all the way round to the road bridge over the canal to get home. He shoved his hands in his pockets, felt the bracelet and looked about. Where had those two girls disappeared to? He was curious about them. He wondered if they needed help.

A noise knocked him out of his thoughts and stopped him in his tracks. He'd heard someone cry out.

Every muscle in Twitch's body was rigid as his heart hammered against his ribs and he listened. He looked about, hoping to see an officer, but they were all behind him, up the path. Should he run and get help? What if it was nothing? What if it was the girls? He decided to take a look. If he saw Robber Ryan, he'd run back shouting the alarm.

Dropping to a crouch, Twitch stealthily made his way through the trees, pausing when he heard voices.

"Shut up, you wuss," said a mean voice.

"I'm sorry," came a whimper.

"The police are everywhere," the mean voice hissed angrily. "You trying to get us in trouble?"

"No, I swear."

Arriving behind a broad oak, Twitch rose, pressing his body against its trunk. Steeling himself, he peeked out. To his surprise, he saw Jack Cappleman about five metres away amongst the trees, facing two notorious bullies from Briddvale College: Richard Peak and Tom Madden. Peaky and Madden, as they were known to all in Briddvale, were dressed in blue tracksuits and wearing white headphones around their necks like jewellery. Madden, the bigger of the two, had his baseball cap on backwards, as if to proudly display the acne that accentuated the fury in his tiny eyes. Peaky was lean, with dark, greasy hair and a cruel smile. He held a lit cigarette and was blowing smoke in Jack's face.

"You're going to find us that money." Madden grabbed Jack by the scruff of his T-shirt. "We want it."

"I don't know where it is," Jack squealed, looking terrified.

"The police reckon Ryan's here. Stands to reason the money's here too," Madden said. "You don't break out of jail and come to a dump like this unless it's to get your loot."

"Nah. You'd get on an aeroplane to Barbados." Peaky sucked hard on his cigarette, nodding as if he knew about these things.

"You're going to look for that money," Madden ordered, "and when you find it, you're going to give it to us, *or else!*"

"But the police are everywhere," Jack whispered, looking like he desperately wished they'd appear.

There was a certain amount of satisfaction in

seeing Jack being bullied, only an hour after he'd tried to force Twitch to eat a worm, but these were older boys and they had a reputation for hurting people. Twitch considered creeping away and leaving Jack to his fate, but he knew his grandad wouldn't have approved. He used to tell Twitch that if he found himself in a situation where he didn't know what to do, he should do whatever would make him feel proud later, even if it was difficult. Twitch knew that if he left Jack in the hands of Peaky and Madden, they would hurt him.

"So do it tomorrow morning," Peaky said. "Round up your gang of plebby schoolmates and search the woods."

"But what if they don't want to?" Jack whined. "It's the summer holidays."

"I don't care." Madden shook Jack. "This is five million quid we're talking about. You're going to search every inch of this place till you find that money, or I'll break every one of your fingers."

Peaky laughed cruelly. "I hope some of your friends can swim."

"Yeah, look in the pond and the river," Madden said, letting go of Jack, who stumbled backwards.

"Unless you don't want to help us?" Peaky threw his

cigarette on the ground and stamped on it, looking at Jack as if he was next.

"I do," Jack whimpered. "I will."

It was the smouldering stub that spurred Twitch into action. It was one thing for Peaky to suck toxic smoke into his body, but to dump the butt on the ground and poison the soil, or a living creature, was too much.

As Twitch hurried back to the path, he heard Jack begging.

"Please don't hurt me. I'll find the money."

"Yes, Officer," Twitch called out loudly, cupping his hands around his mouth so his voice would carry. "I heard voices this way. Over there, through the trees. Do you think it could be the escaped robber?" He crashed towards them making as much noise as possible, grabbing a stick and whacking at the undergrowth.

By the time he reached Jack, Peaky and Madden were gone.

Jack stared at Twitch, then looked past him for the police officers before realizing there were none. His expression changed from shock to confusion that Twitch had helped him. Then he scowled, realizing that Twitch must have seen him being bullied by Peaky and Madden.

Twitch thought Jack was going to say something, perhaps thank you, but instead he turned and ran away through the trees.

Picking up the cigarette butt, Twitch wondered if he was going to regret helping Jack. He hadn't looked grateful. He'd looked angry.

CLARTY CAT

Twitch ran up to his battered blue front door, slipped his key into the lock and let himself in.

"I'm home," he called, dropping his rucksack and lifting off his binoculars, hanging them over the banister as he went into the kitchen. "Mum? Have you heard? A robber has escaped from prison and the police think he's in Briddvale."

"Hello, pet, how was school?" Twitch's mum, Iris Featherstone, smiled at him from the old leather armchair. The shadows around her eyes showed she was tired from her shift at the Elderberry Care Home. She still had on her light blue work tunic. A blaze of evening sunlight streamed through the window behind her, crowning her fine grey-blonde, scraped-back hair with a halo. She looked like a benevolent angel. Her hands were cupped around a steaming mug of tea and her bare bunion-blighted feet were resting on the lumpy footstool.

"School was brilliant," Twitch said, filling a glass from the tap, "because it finished." He downed the water, suddenly realizing how thirsty he was. Leaning over the sink to the window ledge, he switched the radio on. A tune was playing so he turned the volume down and said, "A robber has escaped from Dovelock Prison. The police are searching Aves Wood." He checked the clock. It was nearly six thirty. "Do you think it will be on the news?"

"Aves Wood?"

"I went there after school. There was a police helicopter, and an officer sent me home. He said we should lock all the windows and doors."

"Oh dear!" His mum blinked, looking dazed. "That's a bit frightening."

"Don't worry. I'll protect you."

"Thanks, pickle." She smiled warmly.

"I can make dinner, if you like?" Twitch offered. "If the chickens have been laying, we could have omelette and chips."

"Omelette and chips sounds lovely, and we've plenty of eggs. But I'll make it, pet. You see to the birds."

Twitch pointed at the machine-gun-sized orange

water pistol that was leaning against the armchair. "You're nearly out of ammo."

"When I got home from work, I'd just put my feet up, when Clarty Cat came nosing around." She scowled. "He's after the blue-tit chicks. They're vulnerable, being so close to fledging."

"I hate that cat," Twitch muttered, scanning the high wall that enclosed their back garden.

"Well, today he got a soaking." Her blue eyes twinkled proudly as she took a sip of tea. "He'll not be coming back in a hurry."

Twitch grinned. "Nice one, Mum."

The radio issued a series of beeps signalling the news headlines. He turned it up, but the doorbell went and so he ran to answer it.

"Twitch!" Amita Inglenook greeted him with a smile as he opened the door. "I come bearing gifts, and compostables." She thrust an old square tin at him, brimming with sweetcorn husks, wilting lettuce and apple cores.

"Brilliant, the chickens will be delighted." Twitch moved backwards to let her in.

"Well, you tell those ladies, I expect them to turn my compost into yummy eggs for breakfast, hmm? No clucking excuses." She shuffled past him in her lilac saree and beige cardigan, cackling at her own joke.

Twitch lived at the end of a row of small terraced houses. Amita shared an adjoining wall and had always been their next-door neighbour. Her house had a mirrored layout to his, but where his house had woodchip wallpaper painted magnolia and furniture they'd inherited from his grandparents, Amita's house was a riot of patterns, curious objects and clashing cushions.

He followed her back through to the kitchen, hurrying to the radio.

"Iris, how are you doing? No, no, don't get up, please. I'll sit down." Amita put her large wicker picnic basket with twin lids on the table, and took out a Tupperware pot.

"My feet ache from doing bed baths today," Iris replied as Amita pulled out a chair, "but I'm fine."

"Shh…" Twitch turned the radio up as loud as it would go and they were silenced by the rounded vowels of the woman reading the news.

"The police are searching for a convicted armed robber, who escaped from Dovelock Prison yesterday afternoon…"

"Are you hungry?" Amita opened the plastic container and offered it to him. "I made kachoris to send to Ramith and Danvir. They miss their amma's cooking. Would you like one?"

Twitch took one of the flattened spicy balls of bread as he listened to the news. Amita's children were all grown up now. They had children of their own. But she still cooked for them, posting them home-baked treats in the hope they'd remember how much they missed her food and visit more often.

"You are too skinny." She poked him gently. "Your chickens are fatter than you are. You're a growing boy. You must eat more."

"Did you hear about the escaped robber?" Twitch nodded at the radio, hoping Amita would stop talking so he could listen.

"Dear me, yes. It is very frightening. That robber could be anywhere – hiding in Briddvale." Her eyes grew wide. "And did you hear that Ryan is a *killer*!"

"Who got killed?" Twitch asked. Amita suddenly had his complete attention.

"Ryan's gang attacked a security van from the bank." She leaned forward, her silver eyebrows raised and her brown forehead creasing as she looked from Twitch to Iris and back to Twitch. "They stole five million pounds!"

"Five million," Twitch echoed, realizing Amita's story matched what Peaky and Madden had been saying in Aves Wood.

"Yes, and Ryan was the worst of them."

"Why?"

"Because, after the robbery, Ryan killed all the other robbers" – she dragged her finger across her throat – "then escaped with the money and hid it."

"Where?"

"Nobody knows. The police never found it. That five million pounds is still out there somewhere. That's quite a treasure hunt, hmm?"

Twitch nodded, thinking about what the police officer in Aves Wood had said. "Sure is."

"Imagine if you found it, Twitch."

"It would be brilliant," he whispered, thinking of the expensive camera with the long lens that he secretly dreamed of owning to photograph birds.

"We would be *rich!*" Amita clapped and Iris laughed at the pair of them. "Take more kachoris." Amita nudged Twitch with the Tupperware pot. "I can tell you're hungry."

"*... it is not known if the convict is armed,*" the newsreader said. "*The public are advised not to approach the escaped prisoner and to report any sightings to the police.*"

"Today I made raspberry jam from my allotment canes." Amita lifted one of the basket's hinged flaps and brought out three pots. "These are for you."

"Oh, lovely," Iris said. "We'll have a dollop in our rice pudding tonight."

"But, whilst I was making the jam, I had an accident." Amita opened the basket's other flap, glancing at Twitch before she lifted out an ocean-blue teapot decorated with an ornate gold pattern of star-like flowers.

"Oh, Amita, your beautiful teapot!" Iris cried. "What happened?"

"I was sterilizing the jam jars and dropped one onto my teapot. It sheared the handle right off. A teapot is no use without a handle." She held it out to Twitch. "I thought you might like it for your collection."

He took it reverently and set it down on the kitchen counter. "Thank you."

Twitch had long admired Amita's big blue teapot. It would be the prize pot of his collection. He lifted the lid. The broken handle was inside. "Don't you want to glue the handle back on? I could do it for you."

"Goodness me, no. It's not safe! What if the glue were to give when the pot was full, hmm? I could drop a pot of scalding hot tea on my legs. Burns are terribly slow to heal. I'm too old to live so dangerously."

"I'll hang it in the tree tomorrow," Twitch promised, smiling at his mum.

"It will give me great pleasure to look from my window and see it feeding the birds," Amita said.

"Amita, I wanted to ask you a favour. The girls from work have invited me out on Tuesday. Would you be able to keep an eye on Twitch for me?"

"Mum! I'm twelve years old," Twitch protested. "I don't need a babysitter."

"Don't worry, I won't cramp your style." Amita winked at Iris. "Have you got plans for your summer, Twitch? Any big parties? Hmm?"

"I'm going to train my pigeons," Twitch replied, emptying the tin of scraps into a bucket by the back door and returning it to Amita.

"Train them for what? The Olympics?" Amita chuckled.

"To be homing pigeons, and carry messages, like the ones in the Second World War." Twitch's eyes landed on Amita's picnic basket.

"Good! So, on Tuesday, when you want Aunty Amita to come and read you a bedtime story, you send one of your pigeons with a message and I'll bring my spectacles." Amita beamed and Twitch's mum laughed.

But Twitch wasn't listening. "Amita, can I borrow your basket? There's something I want to do tomorrow and it would really come in handy."

Amita pursed her lips. "I'll lend you the basket in exchange for two eggs."

"Deal." Twitch picked up the bucket of scraps. "I'll go feed the chickens and see if there are any freshly laid."

"Be careful out there." Amita waggled her finger at him. "There's a murderer on the loose."

"Yeah, but he's not going to be hiding in our back garden, is he?" Twitch replied, opening the door. "Anyway, we've got the birds to protect us."

6

THE TEAPOT TREE

The teapot tree was an old wild lilac that grew in the middle of Twitch's garden. From its thatch of leaves and white blooms peeked his collection of broken teapots. Some were hung by their handles and stuffed with straw ready for any bird searching for a nesting box; others had holes where there should've been spouts and were filled with birdseed or fat balls. There were sixteen brightly coloured teapots hanging in the tree like exotic fruit; Amita's blue pot would be the seventeenth. The first teapot had been his grandmother's big yellow six-cupper. When the lid had smashed, his mum had cried, and so Twitch had announced they should hang it in the lilac tree as a bird feeder, in loving memory of Maude Featherstone. Over time other teapots had joined it. Now, when his mum looked at the teapot tree her face lit up with a smile that made Twitch's soul lift like a red kite on an updraught.

As he passed under the tree with his bucket of scraps, Twitch scanned the branches for a spot to hang Amita's teapot. He thought it would make a good drinking fountain, if he secured the lid below the spout to catch rainwater. A cool breeze tousled his hair and he suddenly shivered, his eyes darting to the shadowy parts of the garden, checking for men in black masks. He knew there was no one hiding in the bushes, but his mind was alert and jumpy. He stopped still as a thought popped into his head. Amidst the drama of Aves Wood, he'd forgotten about Billy. Billy, a stranger, who'd appeared in Briddvale that very day, and asked him for an *out of the way* place to park his van. He felt this was a suspicious coincidence. Could Billy be something to do with Robber Ryan? He'd been wearing a hat. Was there a shaved head underneath it? Was *he* the escaped criminal?

As he walked to the end of the garden, he ran through the events that had taken place that afternoon: Billy scaring away Jack and the others, helping him to his feet, chatting about birds, going into the newsagent's to buy the newspaper and Fruit Gums. He hadn't seemed like a robber or a murderer. Twitch had liked him.

Opening the gate to the chicken run, he crossed the bald dirt, broken by rashes of dandelions and a clump or two of grass, and peered into the brick outhouse. Once a toilet, it was now the chicken coop. The hens were shut in every night to keep them safe from predators. Twitch was five when his grandad had taken out the lavatory, installing shelves and nesting boxes for their first chickens. He remembered it fondly. Reaching in, he collected two eggs, one fawn and one a dark beige.

It struck Twitch that there were only two things that were odd about Billy: the first was him asking about somewhere to park his camper van, and the second was him talking to old Mr Bettany about the weather and the state of the roads when his newspaper headline provided a much more interesting and current topic for conversation.

Had Billy purposely steered the conversation so as not to have to talk about Robber Ryan's escape?

Fandango, a rust-coloured chicken with a buff breast and feathered shanks that looked like boots, strutted towards him, her scarlet wattle wobbling. She got her name from the way she moved, performing a Spanish dance of wing flaps, head jerks and claw stomps.

Dodo, Twitch's fat red hen, was hunkered down in a wheelbarrow of straw. Her beetle-black eyes were fixed on the bucket he was carrying. Dodo was lazy. If a fox ever got into the enclosure, she'd be dead in an instant. Even her squawks were lacklustre. The only thing that made Dodo move fast was the rain. She hated getting wet.

Eggbum, the oldest and Twitch's most beloved chicken, whose name came from her being a great layer of eggs, was sat in a terracotta plant pot of soil, growling with pleasure as she gave herself a dust bath. She fluffed up her white feathers, kicking a cloud of dirt over her head and fleshy red comb.

"OK, ladies, grub's up." Twitch shook the bucket as he went to their trough.

Fandango ran with jerky strides, zigzagging to his side. Dodo clucked, barely bothering to flap her wings as she tumbled gracelessly from the wheelbarrow.

"There's plenty for everyone," he said as he poured the scraps into the trough. "Come on, Eggbum, it's supper time." Fandango and Dodo pecked hungrily at the food; Eggbum took her time coming over.

On a hunch, Twitch went over to the pot where she'd been having her bath. "Bingo." He picked up the warm pale oval, adding it to the two in his left hand, and a thought struck him that made him gasp. When he'd been telling Billy about Aves Wood, they'd heard police sirens. Billy had glanced over his shoulder and then suggested they go into the newsagent's.

Billy hadn't wanted to buy him sweets – he'd wanted to get off the street until the police had gone!

Twitch was unsettled by this thought and uncertain what to do about it. Returning to the kitchen, he said nothing, not wanting to worry his mother, and knowing she'd tell him off for talking to a stranger. He showed Amita the three eggs, saying, "All the girls laid today."

Amita pushed her picnic basket across the table and held her hands out for the eggs. "We have a deal," she said happily as Twitch handed her two of the eggs.

Grabbing the basket, he made his excuses, and hurried up the stairs to the bathroom. He needed to establish the facts of the case in his head.

Billy wanted to park his van somewhere free and private.

Billy seemed to be avoiding the police by entering the newsagent's.

Billy might have steered the conversation away from Robber Ryan.

None of these things were a crime, and Billy had saved him from eating a worm. Twitch sighed. If the man was something to do with the escaped convict, the police would catch him. There was nothing he could do.

Instead he'd concentrate on his plan to train his squabs.

When training pigeons Twitch knew it was important to get them to recognize home as soon as they were old enough to fly, but too weak to fly well, or they would disappear into the sunset. Older pigeons weren't trainable. One of the reasons Scabby had stuck around was his injuries, and the free food. Pigeons were intelligent birds.

Putting the picnic basket on the floor, Twitch picked up a small blue watering can and filled it from the bathroom tap. Clambering out of the window onto the flat kitchen roof, he pictured Mum and Amita looking up at the sound of his feet above their heads. The wardrobe-come-pigeon-loft had four stubby legs and stood to the left of the window, against the brick wall. Twitch had spent his Easter holiday building it. In two of the four wooden crates that he'd bolted inside the wardrobe to make nesting boxes sat a pair of pigeons: Scabby and Maud in one, Frazzle and Squeaker huddled together in another. "Come on, squabs," he said softly through the mesh in the door, "time to stretch your wings. Let's teach you to use the trapdoor" – he put his hand through the cat flap-like hole at the top of the door – "so you can get in by yourselves."

He unlatched the wardrobe door and opened it

wide. Maude shot out over his shoulder like a missile. Leaving the door open, Twitch sat down, stretching out his legs, enjoying the heat radiating from the black bitumen roof. He watched Maude circle as she climbed, getting smaller and smaller, and his thoughts turned to Jack Cappleman. What had he done to get on the wrong side of Peaky and Madden? Twitch almost felt sorry for him, but then he remembered the worm.

"Go on," he said to the two squabs cowering in the wardrobe. "Go join your mum."

As if hearing him, Squeaker, the paler of the two, gave a tentative flap of her wings and launched herself up, swimming through the air towards her mother.

Looking utterly disinterested in flying, Scabby fluttered down to the roof beside Twitch and pecked his shoe.

"I'm not feeding you till you've had some exercise. Go on. Go and fly about a bit; you're getting fat." Scabby stared at him, then gave him another peck. Twitch laughed. The sound startled Frazzle, who fell out of the nesting box, snapped out his wings and careered up into the sky.

"All right, Scabby." The bird was tugging at his shoelace with his beak. "You win, but don't tell the others." Twitch prised off the lid of the tub beside the pigeon loft and grabbed a fistful of seed. Scabby fluttered up, perching on his wrist and pushing his beak greedily into the gaps between Twitch's fingers.

As Twitch fed Scabby, he watched the pigeons reeling around one another in the sky. He wouldn't be able to go to Aves Wood tomorrow, unless the police caught Ryan tonight. But he could still take the squabs out for their first homing flight. He hoped they were ready. Amita's basket was the perfect way to carry them. He'd put them in the basket, secure the lids and strap it to his bike. He had to cycle a mile from the loft to release them. The thought of either bird not making it home made his stomach lurch. Instead, he thought about where the five million pounds might be hidden. Imagine if if it was in Aves Wood.

Frazzle landed clumsily in the giant terracotta saucer that served as a bird bath. The doolally bird had big unblinking eyes, a scraggly thin neck and permanently ruffled feathers.

"Look, lads," Twitch said as Frazzle hurried over, "if Robber Ryan comes here, you're going to have to help me defend the house." Scabby carried on eating, but Frazzle stared at Twitch. "Frazzle, if Ryan breaks in, I'll do this." Twitch lifted his chin, pursed his lips and made a warbling whistle. "That will be your signal to attack." Frazzle cocked his head, looking confused. "Like this." Twitch made the whistling sound again, then squawked, flapped his arms and pretended to peck an imaginary person. "Robber Ryan will run away because of your ferocious battle moves, and you'll be rewarded with…" He sprinkled birdseed into his own mouth. "Mmm, yummy." He looked at Frazzle. "What do you think?" Frazzle looked hypnotized. "You have a go." Twitch tipped his head back and whistled. Frazzle stared at him and pooped a white puddle onto the roof.

"Some use you are." Twitch shook his head. "Pigeons are supposed to be clever." He turned to Scabby, who was still guzzling grain. "Scabby, when Frazzle attacks the robber, your job is to fly to the police with a message that I'll write on a scrap of paper and fasten to your leg in one of these." From his pocket, he pulled a tiny silver canister looped onto a Velcro strap.

"Dinner!" his mum called up the stairs.

"Coming," Twitch shouted back, scattering the remaining grain over the roof and dusting off his hands. Lifting the feed bucket lid, he took out the scoop and piled grain into the two bowls in the pigeon loft. With his watering can, he filled the water dishes and the bird bath. Then, ducking in through the window, he washed his hands in the bathroom sink. As he lathered soap over his fingers and thumbs, he thought about Billy and Robber Ryan. Could they be the same person? Surely someone would've recognized him?

Amita had left, and two plates of omelette, chips and salad sat on the table. "This looks great," Twitch declared, sliding into his chair and grabbing his knife and fork.

"Tomorrow is the first day of your holidays," his mum said, cutting into her omelette and letting the steam out. "What're you going to do with it?"

"After my paper round I was going to go to Aves Wood, but I don't think I'll be able to now." Twitch dipped a chip in the gloopy splodge of ketchup on his plate.

"I think you should steer clear of Aves Wood." His mum caught his eye. "You could invite a friend or two over if you wanted. I wouldn't mind. I'd stay out of the way."

Twitch shrugged. The idea of anyone from school coming to his house filled him with horror. He'd built a shield against the jeers in the playground based on the fact that no one really knew him. He didn't want people coming here. It would give them ammunition. His home life was private. He was happy on his own, building his hide, watching the birds and training his pigeons. You knew where you were with birds;

they were better friends than humans. But he didn't say this to his mum. He knew she worried about him not having friends.

When they'd finished, Twitch cleared the plates, whilst Mum dished up the rice pudding and dolloped Amita's jam into it. They took their bowls outside and sat cross-legged on the grass beneath the lilac tree. It was a warm evening and they ate their pudding, watching the sun go down, and discussing the placing of Amita's teapot.

"Give me your bowl," his mum said, getting to her feet. "I'm going to turn in. I've an early start tomorrow."

"I'll put the birds to bed and lock up," Twitch replied, standing up and kissing her on the cheek. "Night, Mum."

After chasing the chickens into their coop and shutting up the pigeon loft, Twitch made his way through the house, closing every window and double-checking the doors were locked. There was only one window he couldn't shut, and that was in his bedroom. Before going up to bed, he went into the living room and took the iron poker from beside the fireplace.

Just in case I need a weapon, he thought.

7

BIRD BOX BED

The staccato bleeps of his alarm woke Twitch at four thirty. He sat up, turned it off and the fairy lights on. Feeling around, he grabbed the clothes he'd set out at the end of his bed – faded jeans, black vest, and oversized camo shirt with poppers instead of buttons – and put them on. Crawling out of the circular door in his box bed, he took the balled-up socks from inside his trainers, pulled them on and shoved his feet into the shoes without undoing the laces. He stretched and his knees cracked as he turned to look out of the window. The sky was aubergine.

Twitch's bed was like a cabin. When he was little, he'd fantasized about being a bird. He loved making himself wings, from cardboard, from his mother's scarves, and once from a pair of kites. Instead of building dens or forts, he'd construct bird boxes with nests inside, and played at being a bird. For his seventh birthday, his grandad had constructed a giant wooden bird box to put over his bed and painted it sky blue. Over the years, Twitch had papered the inside with pictures torn from wildlife magazines, added a shelf for his books, a curtain to draw across the door, and fairy lights. It was his nest and he felt safe inside.

The only other furniture in his room was a chest of drawers. The ceiling, walls and floorboards were painted white. At the far end was a sash window, wedged open at the top with a piece of wood. There were splatters of muck on the wall and floor around the window, because, every summer, Twitch shared his bedroom with a family of swallows.

At the end of March, Twitch would scan the skies every morning, hoping to see the long-tailed birds that flew from South Africa, over the Sahara Desert, to nest in his bedroom. Their arrival heralded the start of the summer. This year Mr Swallow had arrived on the second of April and Mrs Swallow appeared a week later. After a brief courtship, they'd set about building a nest, using mud from Amita's pond, next to an old nest from last year, attached to the architrave beside his window.

Twitch loved to watch them from his box bed. He kept a diary of their activity, as they reared their first brood and the chicks fledged. Now there was a second clutch of eggs in the nest. He was always careful to be calm and quiet around the swallows, and he fancied that they knew and trusted him.

Creeping along the landing to the bathroom, Twitch opened the window, climbed out and silently removed the bird food from the pigeon loft. He was reading a book about training pigeons, and it said not to feed them before their first flight home. Hungry birds would fly straight to the loft for food.

Once in the kitchen, he made himself a bowl of cereal, opened the back door and sat on the doorstep to eat it. The air was moist, but he could tell it was going to be another sunny day. A blackbird called, and a moment later the territorial recitative of a robin answered. He closed his eyes as birds hidden in treetops and shrubberies began their pee-weeting and cooing, tee-weeting and hooting. He recognized the distinctive trill of a wren, then a warbler. He had learned to listen to birdsong, memorizing their calls, and loved being able to identify which birds were around him even when he couldn't see them. It made him feel part of the avian world. As their arias became a chorus, tremolos and trills blending and crescendoing, the sun was summoned from its slumber to rise into the sky again.

Twitch watched the sky change colour as he listened.

"Miss you, Grandad," he whispered, before taking his bowl back inside.

He put the kettle on and made his mum a cup of tea. Tiptoeing upstairs, he left the tea on her bedside table and planted a kiss on her forehead. Creeping out of the house, he pulled on his helmet and unlocked his bike.

The sky was awash with blues and violets as the sun chased the night away. Riding a bike at this time of the day was the best, because there was no traffic. Pedalling hard through the sleeping streets, Twitch built up speed until he reached the downward slope of the main road. He rose up, standing on his pedals and throwing his arms wide. The wind blew his shirt open, so it flapped behind him like a cape as he freewheeled down the hill. He arrived at the newsagent's breathless and grinning as Mr Bettany was unbolting the shutters and opening the door.

"Morning, Twitch." Mr Bettany smiled, crinkling his leathery skin. "You're early."

"It's the first day of the summer holidays," Twitch said, propping his bike against the wall and following him into the shop, where stacks of newspapers bound with string were piled on the floor in front of the counter.

Mr Bettany pointed at the piles. "Need you to sort them into the rounds."

"No problem." Twitch sank to his knees and, taking his penknife from his pocket, cut the string tying the first bundle. Mr Bettany handed him pen and paper, and he began making up the first round. Mr Fullester at number 23 had *The Times*, Mrs Glengarick at number 24 had the *Guardian*, and so on.

Twitch didn't have time to read any of the articles, but it was impossible not to notice that Robber Ryan was on the cover of every newspaper.

RYAN ON THE RUN!

ROBBER RYAN WREAKS HAVOC!

ROZZERS ROCKED BY RYAN!

The papers were all carrying a shadowy picture taken from a petrol station CCTV camera, which showed the back of a figure in a long black coat with a shaved head. The image was grainy, but it was clearly not Billy and Twitch felt relieved. The caption said Ryan had been spotted at a twenty-four-hour garage in Briddvale late on Thursday night. Twitch thought back to what the police officer had said about a sighting and wondered why they thought he'd be heading for Aves Wood.

Whilst making up the newspaper rounds, Twitch glimpsed sentences piecing together the story. A year ago, Ryan had been one of five masked raiders who'd held up a security van at gunpoint. They had stolen five million pounds, the biggest cash theft since the Great Train Robbery. Three of the robbers had been caught and convicted; the fourth had been killed by Ryan, who made off with all the money. Ryan was arrested, pleaded innocent but was found guilty. The police found no trace of the five million pounds. It had never been recovered.

Mrs Inglenook was exaggerating, Twitch thought as he took the remaining newspapers to the empty racks and filled the display. Ryan didn't kill the whole gang, just one member.

"Do you recognize the garage?" Mr Bettany asked, seeing Twitch looking at the papers.

"What?"

"That garage in the picture is the one on Briddvale Road by Aves Wood."

Twitch looked at the picture and felt a jolt as he realized Mr Bettany was right.

Mr Bettany looked at his watch. "Sarah's late again."

"Do you want me to take the north rounds today?" They were the furthest from the shop but if he was quick – which he always was – he could get them done in under two hours and race back home to prepare for his squabs' first homing flight.

"You're a good lad, Twitch." Mr Bettany nodded. "But don't stop to talk to any strangers, mind. Not with that robber about."

"I won't." Twitch picked up the north rounds, sliding them into two canvas delivery bags which he wore criss-crossed across his chest, and set off on his bike, wobbling, weighed down by the newspapers. He peddled to the crossroads at the heart of Briddvale and dismounted. Wheeling his bike over the ditch that ran along the road, he squeezed through a gap in the hedgerow, laid his bike on the ground and removed one of the newspaper bags. It was quicker and easier to do one bag at a time, so on dry days he hid one under the hedge while he did the other. He was pushing it into the well-worn nook when he heard familiar voices and squatted down out of sight.

"Hi." It was Jack Cappleman.

"Why did we have to meet this early?" came the

whining tones of Pamela Hardacre. "Couldn't we have done this later? I have a skincare regime I need to follow, or I'll get spots. It's hard work looking this perfect, you know."

"I told you, we need to go early to get a head start," Jack said. "We're not going to be the only people hunting for that money."

"What are we looking for?" Terry Vallis asked.

"Five million pounds," Jack replied. "Dad says the police think it's in Aves Wood. That's why they were searching it yesterday."

"Yeah, but how big is five million?" Terry asked as they approached the spot where Twitch was hiding. "Is it, like, suitcase big? Or is it the size of a tea chest, or a car? Or a briefcase? It's not going to be sitting in a pile amongst the trees, is it? It'll be buried, or sunk in the pond. I mean, it could be anywhere."

"I don't know where it is." Jack sounded frustrated. "We'll keep our eyes open for signs of digging or disturbed earth; anything that looks suspicious."

"But if the robbery was a year ago, and the money's been hidden in Aves Wood all this time, wouldn't someone have found it by now?" Terry pointed out.

"What if we find a shallow grave in the woods?" asked a soft voice. Twitch peered through the hedgerow, making out the long dark hair and brown eyes of Tara Dabiri. Despite being friends with Pamela, Tara never joined her when she called him names. He shifted to see her more clearly and trod on a stick that snapped loudly.

Tara turned her head, looking right at the spot in the hedgerow where he was hiding. "What was that?"

Twitch froze and held his breath.

"Trust Tara to turn this expedition into a horror movie," Pamela scoffed, giggling and giving her friend a shove. She looked squarely at Jack. "I'm not digging up any skeletons."

"We're not looking for dead people," Jack reassured her. "C'mon, let's go."

"Wait, what about Vernon and Oz?" Terry asked. "Aren't they meeting us here? Vernon's the best at digging."

"Vernon's working; Oz is fishing with his dad."

"Wish I was fishing," Terry muttered as the four of them drifted away, heading south towards Aves Wood.

Twitch let out the breath he'd been holding, remaining where he was until he was sure they'd gone. So Peaky and Madden's threats had frightened Jack into getting a search party together.

Lifting his bike back through the hedgerow, Twitch set off on the first paper round, his bag getting lighter as he went. As he peddled, he thought about places where Ryan might have hidden the money. Twitch knew Aves Wood like the back of his hand. He went there most days after school. He thought back over the past year but couldn't recall a time when he'd noticed disturbed earth or anything that might have been newly buried.

There were a lot of police vehicles on the road this morning, although none of them had their sirens on. Twitch guessed they were widening their search for Robber Ryan, and if Jack planned on going to Aves Wood, it had to be open to the public again.

When Twitch eventually arrived back at the newsagent's, he saw the other rounds had gone. Mr Bettany was serving a customer, so Twitch hovered until he was done.

"I've finished." He pushed the canvas bags across the counter.

"Fastest newspaper boy I've ever had." Mr Bettany handed over a small brown envelope. "Here's your earnings."

"See you next Saturday."

The bell rang as Twitch left, but its reverberations hadn't fallen silent before he was back on his bike and heading home to his pigeons.

MAIDEN FLIGHT

Dropping his bike in the front garden, Twitch didn't bother to ring the bell. His mum would have left for work already so he let himself in with his key. Running up the stairs two at a time, he dashed through the bathroom and climbed out the window. He'd waited nearly two months for this. Setting Amita's picnic basket on the roof in front of the pigeon loft, he opened the wardrobe door and gently, but firmly, wrapped his hands around Squeaker, lowering her into the basket. Then he did the same with Frazzle. There was some fluttering and cooing from the birds, but they were used to being handled by Twitch and weren't alarmed. He tied a bit of string through the basket lids to make sure they stayed shut until he was ready to release the birds. He filled the bowls in the loft with seed, and then put a handful in one of his trouser pockets, just in case.

Siskin Lock was about a mile from his house. Twitch planned to release the birds there. The lock was only a stone's throw from Aves Wood, so he thought, after he'd let the pigeons go, he would see if the police were still there. He was worried that they might have found his hide. The thought of it being smashed apart made him feel ill.

Twitch waved at Mrs Swallow, sat in her nest incubating her eggs, as he grabbed his rucksack from the top of his bed box. It was already ten o'clock. If he was going to venture into Aves Wood, he'd need to take lunch. He went down to the kitchen, grabbed a banana from the fruit bowl and made himself a jam sandwich, putting the food and a flask of water into his bag.

He felt like there was a tiny bird fluttering about inside his chest, trapped by his ribcage. He was excited, but also nervous about what he would do if one of the birds didn't make it home.

Cycling slowly so as not to upset Squeaker or Frazzle inside the basket, which was strapped to his pannier rack with a bungee cord, Twitch made his way carefully down to the canal and along the towpath. Getting off, he pushed the bike as a couple with three dogs came towards him. The dogs were intrigued by the smell of the birds. Twitch stood protectively in front of the basket, as their owners pulled them away.

When he reached Siskin Lock, Twitch removed the basket from the bike, waiting until a group of women in running gear had huffed and puffed their way past and the coast was clear. Taking a breath to calm himself, he untied the string with shaking hands and opened the lid. Squeaker and Frazzle looked up at him, confused. Squeaker opened her beak and a high-pitched chirrup told him she wasn't happy about travelling by basket.

"It's time to fly home," Twitch said calmly, even though his pulse was racing. He reached into the basket and lifted out Squeaker. "If you fly straight back to the loft, there's food waiting for you. Don't take too long or Scabby will eat it all." He gently tossed the bird into the sky. She snapped open her wings, flew in a wide circle, then took off in the direction of home. Twitch smiled as he gazed up at Squeaker cutting a path across the sky and wished for the thousandth time that he had wings.

Frazzle seemed quite happy to stay in the basket and cooed in alarm when Twitch lifted him out. Repeating the action he'd used to release Squeaker, Twitch launched Frazzle into the air, but the bird flapped his wings twice and flew straight to a tree hanging over the other side of the canal.

"Go home, Frazzle." Twitch waved his arms at the bird. "Go on. Shoo. Follow Squeaker."

Frazzle just stared at him, goggle-eyed, from his perch in the tree, so Twitch pushed the lock gates shut and crossed the canal. Picking up a stick, he stretched up, but the bird flew off before he could knock it against the branch.

Frazzle flapped about, zigzagging, then shot off towards Aves Wood.

"Oh no." Twitch dropped the stick. This was what he'd dreaded would happen.

"Why were you poking that bird?" asked a voice, and Twitch saw that the girl with the puffball ponytail and yellow tutu was on the opposite bank of the canal. "That's mean."

"No, no, that's my bird. I wouldn't hurt him. He's my pet. His name's Frazzle." Twitch crossed back over the lock gate. "He was meant to fly home, but he didn't; he flew that way. See, this is his basket."

"What are you going to do?" The girl looked at the basket, intrigued.

"Try and find him, I guess."

"One bird in all those trees." She turned towards the woods. "That's going to be hard." And Twitch realized with a sinking feeling that she was right.

"Are you on holiday?" he asked. "You don't live around here, or I'd know. I've lived in Briddvale all my life."

"No, I'm—"

"Tippi! What have I told you about wandering off?"

Twitch turned and saw Tippi's big sister striding towards them.

"Uh-oh," Tippi whispered. "Ava's cross."

"She was trying to help me catch my pigeon," Twitch said.

Ava shot him a hostile look. "C'mon, Tippi, we've got to go." She held out a hand and Tippi ran to her and took it.

"Wait!" Twitch put his hand in his pocket, realizing as he did so that he was wearing his jeans, and the silver kingfisher bracelet was in his school trousers. "You were in Aves Wood yesterday…"

"No, we weren't." Ava scowled at him. "We just arrived today. We're on holiday with our nan."

Twitch fell silent, shocked that she'd lied to him. Ava whispered angrily to Tippi as the two girls walked away, telling her off. There was something suspicious about those two.

Strapping the empty basket to his bike, Twitch turned around, scanning the forest canopy for his dozy-looking pigeon. He cupped his hands around his mouth and made pigeon noises, but nothing moved. He threw his head back and made the warbling whistle he'd sung the previous evening on his roof, and suddenly he caught sight of a bird with the characteristics of Frazzle a way up the canal, swooping clumsily down behind Crowther Bridge. He jumped onto his bike and pedalled as fast as he could, trying to keep the pigeon in sight.

When he reached the other side of the bridge, there was no sign of the errant pigeon. He continued on to the west gate into Aves Wood. A sign saying bicycles were not allowed was bolted to the gate. He took off the basket and pretended to check his tyres, making sure no one was coming. Opening the gate, he quickly pushed it through, wheeling his bike off the path and onto the track into the woods, hurrying to a pile of sticks and bracken. Glancing over his shoulder, he lifted the biggest stick, bringing up a tapestry of woven ferns. He'd made the secret bike park back in the spring. He laid his bike down on the ground, and let the blanket of ferns fall, hiding it from view.

The nature reserve was busy. Curious locals had come to gawp and officers in pairs were still patrolling the main paths. Twitch took out his binoculars, searching branch after branch for his renegade squab. Not only was he worried about Frazzle but he was growing increasingly anxious about his hide. He decided to head in that direction as he searched for Frazzle. He tried not to panic about the pigeon. His book had said that birds might not immediately fly home, particularly on their first homing flight.

As Twitch approached the pond, the knot in his stomach tightened as he prepared himself for the sight of a demolished hide. But when he reached the clearing, there were no signs of anyone having been there. It was exactly as he'd left it. He yanked the coat hanger to open the door and crawled inside.

Safe in his forest hideout, Twitch took out his jam sandwich and felt a flash of pride as he ate his lunch. The police had combed the woods and not found his hide.

Once his hunger was sated, he secured the hide and set out again, hunting for Frazzle. He'd covered nearly half the woods without spotting his bird, when he heard a mean laugh and a voice he recognized as Tom Madden's.

"... I mean, I *want* to punch you, so it's win–win for me."

Everyone knew Madden planned on being a professional boxer. He never missed an opportunity to practise on people who annoyed him. Instantly alert, Twitch moved swiftly through the trees, coming to an abrupt halt as he spied Peaky tying Jack to a tree trunk. Madden was dancing about, punching at the air in front of Jack's face.

"I'll find it." Jack sounded terrified. "We've been looking all morning."

"Really?" Madden feigned an uppercut. "Where are your friends now? Huh?"

"They got bored and went home. I need more time," Jack begged.

"And I need money," Madden replied, suddenly pivoting and punching Jack in the stomach.

Twitch flinched with horror as Jack cried out. He had to do something.

9

ALARM CALL OF A PEREGRINE FALCON

Dropping to the forest floor, Twitch put down Amita's basket and searched for missiles. He couldn't tackle the two boys on his own; they'd make mincemeat of him. He found a stone, but it was too small. The trick he'd used on Jack wouldn't work here. He considered his options and then grinned. Pulling out his penknife, Twitch cut an armful of ferns and held them between him and the boys as he crept in a crouch around the clearing, stopping beside a wide tree a couple of metres behind the bullies.

Peaky and Madden were laughing at Jack, who was crying and promising to give them twenty quid from his savings if they'd leave him alone. Slowly rising to his feet, ferns shielding him, Twitch stabbed his penknife into the tree trunk at head height, then dropped back to the ground. He peeped through the

82

ferns to see if his actions had attracted attention, but none of the boys had noticed him.

Now for phase two, he thought as he moved quickly and quietly, edging around the small clearing until he was behind the tree that Jack was tied to. Finding a dense patch of undergrowth, Twitch lined himself up with the penknife, parted the bracken and lay down on his back, covering himself. He glanced up at the forest canopy and prayed for wood pigeons and a true aim. Drawing in a deep breath, he cupped his hands around his mouth, and as loudly as he could mimicked the dry *kak-kak-kak-kak-kak-kak* alarm call of a peregrine falcon.

The noise was eerie. Peaky and Madden's laughter stopped dead. A cacophony of wing snaps, leaf rustlings and avian cries filled the forest as birds rocketed off their branches in fear.

"What was that?" Peaky asked, grabbing Madden's arm. The two boys looked around in a panic.

"*Kak-kak-kak-kak-kak-kak,*" Twitch called again.

While their heads were turned the other way, he sat bolt upright and threw the stone as hard as he could at his penknife. He scored a direct hit, making the blade vibrate noisily.

Peaky and Madden jumped, suddenly seeing the vibrating blade sticking out of the tree.

"Someone threw a knife at us!" Peaky yelled.

"Who's there?" Madden shouted boldly, spinning around in a circle, but Peaky was already sprinting away through the trees.

"Run!" Peaky shouted. "It's Ryan! It's *RYAN!*"

Madden bolted after him, stumbling over Amita's basket. Twitch chuckled as he watched the bullies run away, but his smile faded when he got to his knees and saw Jack thrashing about in his bonds, terrified. "It's all right." Twitch stood up. "It's only me." He walked past Jack and pulled his penknife from the trunk of the tree.

Jack gaped at Twitch in shock. His face was wet with tears and a bubble of snot ballooned out of one of his nostrils. He looked around, confused, as if what he was seeing couldn't be real. "Why do you keep helping me?" he whispered, distressed.

"Because you keep needing help," Twitch replied with a shrug. He pointed to the rope binding Jack to the tree. "Want me to untie you?"

Jack's face burned with shame and anger, but he nodded.

Stepping behind the tree, Twitch saw the knots had been tied very tight and the rope was cutting into Jack's wrists. "Keep still." He sliced the cord with his knife and Jack stumbled away from the tree, staring at him suspiciously. "I don't think Peaky and Madden will want you to look for Ryan's loot any more," Twitch said with a wry smile. He put a gentle hand on Jack's shoulder to indicate he should sit, then sat down cross-legged on the ground in front of him, carefully working the knots around Jack's wrists apart, until the rope fell to the forest floor. His wrists were bruised where there was bleeding beneath the skin. His swollen fingers resembled purple sausages. In silence, Twitch took Jack's hands and gently massaged them, like he rubbed his mother's tired feet, until they began to look more normal.

"Why are you being nice to me?" Jack asked quietly.

"Every living thing deserves respect, don't you think? Even vermin."

Jack snatched his hands back, his chin jutting forward. "You calling me vermin?"

"No." Twitch shook his head. "I'm talking about Scabby, the pigeon you wanted to kill. Remember him? You said he was vermin."

"Why are you talking about that pigeon?" Jack looked bemused.

"That's what you reminded me of, when I saw you trapped by those bullies." He shrugged. "I didn't leave him, and I couldn't leave you. They were going to hurt you." He blinked. "Like you were going to hurt Scabby."

"I wouldn't really have killed that pigeon." Jack stared at the ground and Twitch knew he was lying. "It was Vernon's idea."

Twitch said nothing.

"What happened to it? Did it die? It only had one leg. We didn't do that."

"I took him home."

"Really? My mum would freak out if I brought a mangy old pigeon home from school."

"My mum likes birds, and Scabby's happy. He's got a family now."

"Family?"

"Yeah, he's a dad. He's got a wife called Maude and two squabs, Frazzle and Squeaker."

Jack looked at him as if he'd just said that fairies were real and lived in his back garden. Picking up a twig, Jack scored a figure-of-eight pattern in the dirt. "I'm not like Peaky and Madden, you know."

"Aren't you?" Twitch looked blankly at him. "You pick on me. You were trying to get Vernon to kill Scabby. Why d'you do that?"

"I just wanted everyone to think I was tough, you know, that I was cool," Jack muttered.

"You can't *make* people think you're cool."

Jack snorted. "No. *You* can't make people think you're cool."

Twitch shrugged. "Doesn't bother me."

"Bet it does."

"Nope."

"Everyone wants to be liked."

"I don't mind if people don't like me."

"You don't want friends?" Jack asked disbelievingly.

"I've got friends." Twitch glanced up into the branches of the tree that Jack had been tied to. "I'm searching for one now as a matter of fact. Frazzle. The dizzy-witted thing doesn't know north from south."

"A *bird*?" Jack looked amazed.

"Yeah."

"Birds can't be your friends!"

"Why not?"

"Because they're birds!"

"Birds make me happy. They're good company, they help me with school…"

"Oh, come on!" Jack laughed. "Help you with school?"

"They do." Twitch looked at Jack through his fringe. "When teachers explain things, I don't understand the first time, or the second sometimes, but I keep at it, because when I grow up, I need to work with birds."

He picked at a fern frond. "I've got to; it's the only thing I want to do. Mum says to work with birds I need to be good at science, so when I get home from school, I go over everything we did in class to make sure I understand it. Everything you need to know about anything is written in books. If you don't understand something, you can look it up." He stopped, suddenly self-conscious. He'd never talked about this with anyone his own age before and wasn't sure why he was telling Jack.

"But you get good grades!" Jack was surprised. "You're a nerd."

"I've read every book about birds in Briddvale Library," he admitted. "Some of them twice." He leaned back, propping himself on his elbows and staring up into the canopy. "If it wasn't for the birds, I wouldn't see the point in trying. Learning about bird habitats and migration helped me with geography. And when I read about how carrier pigeons were used in the world wars, I was learning history." He smiled. "Listening to the dawn chorus has helped me understand music."

"What's the dawn chorus?"

Twitch sat up. "Have you never listened to the birds sing in the morning?"

"No."

Twitch stared at Jack's blank face in astonishment. "But it's there for you to hear every day. All you have to do is get up early. It's magic."

Jack rubbed his wrists. "You're weird."

"My grandad used to say everyone is weird; they just pretend to be normal."

"No, you are legit weird," Jack said, shaking his head. "Was it you who made that freaky noise that spooked the birds?"

"I mimicked the alarm call of a peregrine falcon. They prey on wood pigeons, so I figured if anything'd send the birds skywards it'd be a peregrine. See, the birds did you a favour."

Jack's eyebrows lifted and he blinked as he thought about this.

"The trouble is, I've probably scared Frazzle away too."

"So, what does this bird friend of yours look like?"

"He's a common pigeon that looks like he's been dragged through a hedge backwards. Oh, and he's daft."

"I thought you said they were rock doves."

"They are," Twitch replied, pleased that he'd remembered.

"I'll help you find it," Jack got to his feet, "as payback."

"All right." Twitch jumped up and went to the spot where he'd left the bird basket, sighing as he saw what was left of the stomped-on wicker remains. If he did find Frazzle, getting him home was going to be tricky.

10

SCABBY'S REVENGE

Twitch and Jack walked through the woods peering up into the branches of every tree.

"We could split up," Jack suggested. "Call each other if we see the pigeon."

"You don't know what Frazzle looks like," Twitch shook his head. "Anyway, I don't have a phone."

Jack stopped. "You don't have a phone?"

"I mean. I have one," Twitch replied. "Just not on me."

"Where is it?"

"In a drawer, at home. I don't use it." He found he was blushing. "There's no signal in Aves Wood."

"Why don't you use it?"

"Only person I'd ring is Mum."

"Look!" Jack's eyes lit up as he pointed. "There, is that Frazzle?"

"That's a blackbird. Don't you know the difference between a pigeon and a blackbird?"

"Sure I do. One's black and one's grey." Jack pointed again. "Look, there. That's a blackbird."

"That's a crow!"

"Same thing."

"A blackbird is a type of thrush; it has a yellow beak and sings. A crow is larger with a black beak and it caws tunelessly. You might confuse a crow with a rook or a raven, because they're all from the corvid family, but a blackbird is totally different."

Jack stopped walking and stared at him.

"What?"

"Corvus, that's your name. It means 'crow', doesn't it? You just said so. Corvus Featherstone. You're named after a crow."

Twitch felt his skin reddening. "My grandad named me."

"After a crow?"

"Corvus means 'crow' or 'raven'. They were the messengers of Apollo..." Twitch's voice petered out as he heard how lame he sounded.

"Oh my goodness!" Jack laughed.

"What?"

"You're this weird, pale, blond vegetarian named

after a gnarly black bird that carries messages for gods and pecks out dead people's eyeballs."

"Eyeballs?"

"I don't know much about birds, but I've seen plenty of zombie movies. And ravens definitely eat corpses."

Twitch grabbed Jack's arm, motioning for him to be silent. Strutting about at the edge of the car park to Aves Wood was a scrawny-looking pigeon.

Is that Frazzle? Jack mouthed silently and Twitch nodded.

Reaching into his pocket, Twitch pulled out some birdseed and made quiet chirping noises as he approached the pigeon slowly, scattering the seed in front of him. Seeing the seed, Frazzle marched towards it. As the bird pecked at the food, Twitch relaxed his body, remaining still for a long moment, aware that Jack was watching him. Waiting until the pigeon was close enough, Twitch cupped his hands around Frazzle, pinning his wings to his body with a swift but gentle movement, and picked him up.

"Frazzle, meet Jack," Twitch said, turning the bird to face him. A van drove into the car park. It had *Horizon News* printed on the side. "Reporters now too?" he grumbled. "There are too many people in Aves Wood. They'll frighten the birds."

"People are going crazy about Robber Ryan. My mum thinks we're all going to be murdered in our sleep. She's made my dad put all her jewels in our bank safe-deposit box."

Twitch wondered if his mum had any jewels. She wore her mother's wedding ring on a chain around her neck, but he didn't think it was valuable. "I wish the police would hurry up and catch Ryan, so everything can go back to normal."

"Don't you think it's exciting?"

"It's ruining the birdwatching."

"But think of all the things you could do if you found five million pounds."

"You wouldn't be able to spend it. You'd have to hand it over to the police."

"They wouldn't miss a million of it."

With both hands holding Frazzle, Twitch had to toss his hair out of his eyes to give Jack a sardonic look. "Then you'd be a thief too."

"Fine, I'd hand it all in, but there's got to be a reward for that much money. We should find out what it is. Hey, we could search for the stolen loot together and split the reward."

"I thought you were looking for the stolen loot with Tara, Pamela and Terry."

"How did you know about that?" Jack shot him an inquisitive glance, then sighed. "They got bored. Does Frazzle mind when you hold him like that?"

"Not any more. I've done it so many times. And I'm not hurting him, just stopping him from flying away again."

"I'd be too scared to hold a bird."

"You'd get used to it."

"I've never picked up one." He peered at Frazzle. "How are you going to get him home?"

"I don't know," Twitch replied. "I cycled here, with Frazzle and Squeaker in that basket Peaky and Madden trampled on. I guess I'll walk home carrying him and come back for my bike tomorrow. I can't let Frazzle go, in case he flies off again."

"I could walk with you," Jack offered, "and wheel your bike."

Twitch felt a flicker of panic at the thought of Jack Cappleman coming to his house. "It's over a mile away. You've probably got other things to do. I'll be fine."

"Not really," Jack admitted. "I was going to spend the afternoon looking for Robber Ryan's millions to try and stop Peaky and Madden from killing me. Hey, I should tell them that the police found me and I had to give a statement about what happened. That should make them leave me alone for a bit." He smiled. "I owe you big time. I don't mind walking your bike home." He looked away, trying to appear unbothered. "I'd kind of like to see that pigeon."

"Scabby?"

"Yeah. What? Why are you looking at me like that?"

"Well, you … you bullied me for saving that pigeon."

"It wasn't because of the pigeon." Jack avoided Twitch's gaze. "You made me look mean and stupid in front of everyone." He paused, and Twitch thought that it hadn't been him who'd made Jack look mean and stupid. "Anyway, that's finished now. You saved me from Peaky and Madden, *twice*! I owe you."

"You don't."

"Please?" Jack's face was open and unguarded. "Let me make things even. I couldn't bear it if I owed you for ever."

"Wheeling my bike home will not make us even."

"It's a start." Jack smiled winningly.

"OK, fine," Twitch replied gruffly.

"Where's your bike then, Corvus?" Jack said with a grin. "Let's go get it."

"It's this way," Twitch said, marching back into the trees clutching Frazzle. "And don't call me Corvus."

When they got to where he'd hidden his bike, Twitch told Jack to lift the bracken cover. As he did, Jack shot Twitch an impressed look, and despite himself, Twitch glowed a little with pride. They passed through the gate out onto the towpath, Jack pushing the bike and Twitch carrying Frazzle.

"There's Billy!" Twitch said, recognizing a figure on the path ahead. "Billy!" he called, hurrying forward.

Billy was wearing a powerful pair of binoculars around his neck and carrying a fancy-looking camera. "Twitch!"

"Are you bird-spotting?" Twitch asked, looking at the binoculars.

"Er, yes. That's exactly what I'm doing. I'm spotting birds." He glanced at Twitch's hands. "What's that you have there?"

"It's my pet pigeon, Frazzle. I'm taking him home."

Billy raised an eyebrow. Then he saw Jack over Twitch's shoulder and his other eyebrow joined it. "What's he doing here?"

"Oh, Jack's OK. We sorted all that worm stuff out. He's doing me a favour and walking my bike home whilst I carry Frazzle."

"Are you sure that's a good idea?" Billy asked, barely moving his lips.

Jack was hanging back, obviously wary of the man who'd chased him away yesterday.

"Yeah, it's fine." Twitch dismissed his concern. "But, you won't see any good birds today. There are too many people about. The birds are all hiding."

"First day of the summer holidays. Bound to be a busy one."

"No. It's that robber who escaped from prison. Everyone's looking for him."

"Are they?"

"People think the money's hidden in Aves Wood. Ryan was spotted at the garage on Briddvale Road on Thursday night."

"Really?"

"Yes." Twitch frowned, surely Billy must have heard the news. "Did Mr Patchem let you park your camper van in his bottom field?"

"He did. Nice feller. That was a good tip, Twitch. Thank you."

"What kind of van have you got?"

"An old orange VW. Stop by for a cup of tea if you want. I'll be there for a few days."

"VWs are the coolest," Twitch said, noticing Billy's eyes darting back to the trees beyond the path. Twitch understood what it was like to want to be left alone to watch the birds. He stepped aside. "We'd better go. Got to get Frazzle back home."

"See you around, lads," Billy said, lifting his binoculars.

The closer Twitch got to his house, the more nervous he felt about letting Jack in.

"It's not far now," he said. "You can leave the bike here if you like. You've more than paid me back."

"Don't you want me to come to your house?" Jack asked.

"It's not that," Twitch lied. "I thought you might have got bored, or want to go home."

They turned onto the short road where Twitch lived and he nodded to the house at the end of the terrace. "That's where I live, the one with the blue door."

Jack nodded, his expression blank. Twitch knew Jack's house was four times the size of his.

"Mum's at work." Twitch looked down at the breast pocket of his camo shirt. His door key was buttoned into it. "Could you get my key out of my shirt pocket and open the door?"

"What should I do with your bike?"

"Lay it on the grass." He nodded to the tiny rectangle of lawn in front of the living room window.

Jack opened the door and Twitch pushed past, climbing the stairs to the bathroom. Jack followed him.

"Can you slide the window up?"

Looking baffled, Jack did as he was asked, and Twitch stepped out onto the flat roof, releasing Frazzle, who fluttered to the landing hatch and strutted through the trapdoor, disappearing inside the loft. Peeping through the mesh in the door, Twitch saw Squeaker and felt a wave of relief. She'd made it home.

"Your pigeons live in a wardrobe?"

"They don't know what a wardrobe is," Twitch said, shaking out his stiff hands.

"Does your neighbour mind you having pigeons?"

"She's not a massive fan of Scabby. She left her bathroom window open once." He pointed to the rectangular window in the adjacent wall. "Scabby flew in and gave her a terrible fright when she was having a bath." Twitch chuckled. "She came to our door in her bathrobe wearing a shower cap and waving a loofah at me. I had to go in and get him out." Jack laughed. "Want to help me feed them?" He opened the tub of seed and the wardrobe door, taking out the silver grain dishes. "Take the scoop."

Jack scooped up some seed. "How much should I give them?"

"Half in each bowl."

Maude flew out, taking the opportunity to exercise her wings. Scabby fluttered down and hopped about the rooftop.

Jack stared at the bird. "Is that him? Is that the one…?"

"Yeah." Twitch sat down, holding his palm flat, sprinkling grain onto it. Scabby hopped, then fluttered onto Twitch's knee, eagerly approaching the food.

"I didn't really want to kill him," Jack said quietly, more to himself than Twitch.

"Here, hold out your hand." Twitch poured a little seed onto it, then held Jack's hand steady beside his. Scabby took a minute or two to move, but eventually he hopped onto Jack's hand and started to eat the seed.

"He's really light," Jack whispered, not wanting to spook the bird.

"He's got hollow bones; most birds do, to help them fly. Pigeons are great flyers; they have these air sacs, like balloons, in their body that fill when they're flying. They're also really smart – well, except for Frazzle."

Jack didn't take his eyes off Scabby. He piled a bit more grain onto his hand and Scabby cooed appreciatively. Maude fluttered down, landing on Jack's knee, and joined Scabby to dine off his hand.

Jack smiled at Twitch. "I think they like me."

Scabby's head jerked back then forwards and back again, before he suddenly regurgitated his food onto Jack's palm.

"*Ewww*, gross!" Jack held his hand away and leaned back. "Scabby puked on me!"

Twitch laughed. "When birds bring up their food, it's a sign of affection."

"They puke on you if they like you?" Jack grimaced.

"Something like that." Twitch giggled as Jack's face contorted with disgust.

"Oh, grim, no! Scabby's pecking at the puke. He's eating it! *He's eating his own sick!*"

Twitch howled with laughter.

"Get him off! Make him stop. Twitch! Stop laughing. I'll be sick myself in a minute." And then Jack started laughing too.

"Scabby's got his revenge!" Twitch hooted.

11

SWALLOW DIVE

The boys were still chuckling as they washed their hands in the bathroom sink. Jack dried his on the towel and wandered out onto the landing. "Is this your bedroom?" he asked, walking forwards and pushing the door open.

"Don't!" Twitch cried, but it was too late. Jack was inside and looking about.

"What's the big blue box? Is this a storage room? Oh! There's a bird's nest up there!"

"Shh." Twitch grabbed Jack's arm to stop him from going too close to the swallows' nest. "There's eggs in there. She's keeping them warm."

"Oh," Jack exhaled, stepping back beside Twitch and staring up at the swallow, who was glaring down at them. "Birds have bedrooms in your house?" he whispered.

"Just in my room. The swallows nest here every summer."

"Every summer?"

Twitch nodded. "Since I was little."

"But..." Jack looked around. "Where do you sleep?"

Twitch paused, wondering if he was going to regret this, and then pointed to the box bed. "In there."

"Really?" Jack dropped to his knees, poking his head through the hole before Twitch could stop him. "This is great," he hissed, scrambling inside.

For a second, Twitch was uncertain what to do. No one but his mum had ever been in his box bed. But he clambered in after Jack and turned on the fairy lights.

"This is like having your own den!" Jack took in the pictures of birds on the walls. "What's this?" He pointed to a hand-drawn map pinned to the wall. "Is it Aves Wood?"

"Er, yeah, it's where I do my birdwatching. It shows the different habitats and places I've spotted rare birds."

"You've mapped every path." Jack studied the map. "You must know the nature reserve like the back of your hand."

"Pretty well, yeah."

"So, if you were going to hide five million pounds in there, where would you put it?"

Twitch knew exactly where he'd hide something he didn't want found. He'd sink it in one of the shallow pools around the pond that looked like land, but he wasn't about to tell Jack that. It was too close to his hide. "Dunno." He shrugged.

Jack narrowed his eyes, sensing Twitch was holding back. "Are you worried I'm going to tell everyone at school that you sleep in a box and let birds puke on you?"

"Are you worried I'm going to tell everyone you made them look for money that you were always going to give to Peaky and Madden, because they own you. And the only reason you know about my birds is because they puked on you?"

Jack grinned. "I won't tell if you don't."

"Deal." Twitch nodded, trying not to smile back.

"Can we look at the swallows?"

"You have to keep your distance. Don't startle them with any loud noises or big movements."

"Don't worry, I won't. I don't want to upset them."

"It's not them I'm worried about – it's you. They'll come for you if they feel threatened. Do you like being dive-bombed and pooped on?"

"Poop's worse than puke," Jack said, shaking his head.

"Then do as I say, and whisper."

They crawled out of the box bed and got to their feet, tiptoeing slowly and quietly to a spot a metre from the nest and looked up at the ceiling.

"How many eggs are in there?" Jack whispered.

"I don't know. It's their second clutch. Usually a swallow will lay four to six eggs. The first clutch was four and I think there's another four up there, but I haven't looked."

"Second clutch?"

"Yeah. They come here to breed, then at the end of the summer the whole family will fly back to Africa."

As they were talking, Mr Swallow flew through the window with an unfortunate insect struggling in his beak. He was bringing food for Mrs Swallow.

"Oh, you have chickens!" Jack whispered, pointing out of the window.

Twitch pulled him back. "Yeah, we've got three."

"And a pet cat."

"What?" Twitch gasped, ducking to peer out of the window and feeling a splat on his head from the protective Mr Swallow.

An ungroomed white cat the size of a small dog was climbing the trunk of the teapot tree with his eyes fixed on the blue-tit nesting box. Twitch yelled at Clarty Cat, who looked disdainfully up at him as Mrs Swallow shrieked, Mr Swallow dived and Jack leaped backwards, crying out in alarm. Twitch dashed out of his bedroom, almost falling down the stairs, and sprinted into the kitchen. Grabbing the giant water pistol, he threw open the back door, yelling and squirting like a berserker.

Clarty Cat hissed, leaping from the tree onto the wall, fixing Twitch with a furious glare, before dropping into the chicken run and sending the hens squawking in circles. Twitch lurched after him, yelling and aiming a jet of water at the spitting, hissing beast. He hit the cat, who yowled, vaulted over the wall and was gone.

"Take this." Twitch handed the water pistol to Jack, who'd caught up with him. "If Clarty Cat comes back, shoot him. I need to check on the girls."

Jack nodded, watching as Twitch opened the gate to the chicken run. Eggbum was in the coop, but Fandango had got herself trapped behind the wheelbarrow and was making a terrible racket. Twitch picked her up and held her gently, murmuring calming noises as he carried her to the coop. He looked about and spotted Dodo cowering under a bush. He lifted the hen from her hiding place and shut her in the coop too.

"Are they all right?" Jack called.

"They're fine. Clarty Cat has scared them silly."

"Clarty Cat is a weird name."

"Clarty means filthy and dirty. Mum named him Clarty Cat because he looks like he could do with a good bath." He walked past Jack, scanning the ground around the lilac tree, and then looked up into the branches. "The blue tits seem OK." He sighed with relief. "Well done for spotting the cat. You probably saved their lives."

"There are teapots in that tree!" Jack stared up at them.

"The chickens won't lay now, not until they've recovered," Twitch said, ignoring Jack's exclamation.

"Twitch, I'm home. I—" Iris Featherstone came out into the garden. "Oh, hello." She glanced at Jack, then at Twitch, then back at Jack, suddenly beaming. "Aren't you going to introduce me to your friend?"

"Mum! Er ... this is Jack. He's in my form at school."

"Hello, Jack." Iris shook his hand, smiling warmly. Twitch felt himself go red at the delight on his mum's face. She pointed to the water pistol. "Clarty Cat?"

Jack nodded. "He was climbing the tree when I spotted him. He jumped in the run with the chickens, but Twitch got him with the water pistol and chased him away." Then he added, "But don't worry. All the birds are OK."

"Thank goodness. Have you eaten?" she asked, and

the boys shook their heads. "Would you like to stay for dinner, Jack?"

Twitch felt panic freeze his muscles. He opened his mouth to speak, but nothing came out.

"We're having toad-in-the-hole with veggie sausages and green beans."

"Jack has to get home," Twitch blurted out at the same time as Jack said, "Yes please, Mrs Featherstone."

They looked at each other.

"Great, that settles it. Dinner for three." Twitch's mum turned round and headed back into the kitchen, pretending that Twitch hadn't spoken.

"I won't stay if you don't want me to," Jack said after a moment of awkward silence.

"It's just … yesterday you were trying to shove a worm in my mouth, and now you're all *yes please, Mrs Featherstone*." He shrugged. "It's … you know, weird."

"Why've you got teapots in your tree?" Jack asked.

"I like them, OK?"

"Aren't you worried that people will laugh?"

"Mum says laughter's a good thing, and people can naff off if they don't like it."

"I've never met anyone like you." Jack folded his arms. "You're … interesting."

"Welcome to the freak show." Twitch waved his

hand at the chickens and up at the pigeon loft. "If you're going to make fun of me to everyone, there's not much I can do about it now."

"I don't want to make fun of you," Jack said feelingly.

"Yeah, well, be nice." Twitch frowned. "If you upset Mum, I'll do more than soak you with a water pistol."

"Does she know about … about school?"

"You bullying me?" Twitch shook his head.

"Right." Jack looked about. "So, what do we do until dinner?"

"You can help me muck out the chickens."

"What?"

Twitch laughed. "You wanted to stay for dinner."

Jack discovered that mucking out the hens was merely a matter of exchanging the straw in their coop for the fresh stuff in the wheelbarrow. Twitch told him what to do and laughed at the delight on Jack's face when he discovered an egg in the hay.

"You'd think it was Ryan's loot, you look that proud," Twitch teased.

Jack took a liking to Dodo, who didn't run away when he petted her, and by the time the boys were washing their hands for dinner they were chatting away about birds as if it was what they always did, except that they both knew it wasn't, and Twitch wondered how much of it was a performance for his mum.

"Would you like gravy, Jack?" Iris asked.

"Yes please."

"You know, I don't think Twitch has ever mentioned you to me. Did you say you were in the same form at school?"

"Yes," Jack replied. "But we don't have many classes together. We only got to know each other recently."

Twitch stuffed a forkful of toad-in-the-hole in his mouth, so he didn't have to say anything.

"How did you become friends?" Iris asked.

"Twitch stopped some older boys from bullying me," Jack replied.

Iris beamed proudly at Twitch. "That sounds like my son."

Twitch tilted his head forward, letting his fringe hide his face.

"I wish you'd told me you were having a friend over," Iris chided Twitch gently. "I'd have got us some pudding."

"It wasn't planned," Jack answered for him. "I bumped into Twitch in Aves Wood. He was looking for Frazzle. I helped him bring the pigeon back. I didn't realize you had so many birds here."

"Yes." Iris chuckled. "We joke that we should call the place The Aviary and put up a sign outside."

"You should," Jack replied enthusiastically, and Twitch hated him a little for his hypocrisy. "Twitch showed me the swallows' nest, and his cabin bed. I wish I had a bed like that."

"Has he taken you to his hide?"

"His what?" Jack looked at Twitch.

"That was delicious, Mum," Twitch said hurriedly. "Is there any more?"

"I'm afraid not, pet. Are you still hungry?"

"No, no. Only, if there was some, I would've eaten it, because, you know, it's my favourite." He pushed his chair back from the table and carried his plate over to the sink. "It's getting late, and I have to see to the pigeons," he said, giving Jack a meaningful look.

Jack put his knife and fork together on his empty plate. "That was wonderful, Mrs Featherstone," he said politely. "I should be heading home. My parents don't know I'm here and they will worry if I'm late back."

"Do you live far?"

"The east side of Aves Wood."

"But that's a couple of miles away. You're not going to walk?"

"He's borrowing my bike," Twitch said.

"I am?" Jack looked at Twitch, who nodded. "Great, then I'll get going. Thanks for having me."

"You're welcome any time, Jack – isn't he, Twitch?"

Twitch rolled his eyes, accompanying Jack to the front door.

"What's your hide?" Jack asked.

"Nothing." Twitch made his expression blank, letting Jack know he wasn't going to say anything more about it.

"Are you sure about me taking your bike?"

Twitch was already regretting his spontaneous offer. "Yeah. It's fine."

"I'll bring it back tomorrow morning, first thing," Jack promised. "What time do you get up?"

"Five."

"In the morning?" Jack looked appalled.

"For the dawn chorus."

"Oh! Right." Jack nodded. "See you in the morning, then."

12

DAWN CHORUS

The sky was violet when Twitch crawled out of his box bed, sleepy-eyed and only half awake. He shoved his feet into his slippers and crept downstairs in his pyjamas. As he approached the bottom of the staircase, he heard a rattle that made his heart jump. His eyes snapped wide and he looked about in fear. The letter box squeaked as it rose, and a pair of eyes stared up at him. He opened his mouth to yell.

"Twitch, it's me," a voice hissed.

His head was foggy with sleep, and it took a minute for Twitch to put the voice and eyes together. "Jack?" he whispered in amazement. "Is that you?"

"Of course it's me. Who did you think it was? Robber Ryan?"

Twitch opened the door. Jack was on the doorstep clutching Twitch's bike, smiling awkwardly.

"Morning!" Jack said.

"What are you doing here? It's five o'clock!"

"I brought your bike back."

"Yeah, but I didn't mean you had to do it first thing." Twitch was stunned. "To be honest, I thought you might not give it back at all."

"I said I would," Jack snapped defensively. "My bike's better than yours anyway…" He stopped himself and sighed. "Sorry." Looking self-conscious, he said, "I wanted to … I mean, I wondered if you'd show me the dawn chorus? You made it sound cool."

Twitch blinked with surprise, wondering who this Jack was and what he'd done with the real Jack Cappleman. He stepped aside. "Leave the bike on the grass and come in, but be quiet. Mum's still asleep."

"Nice pyjamas."

"Shut up. It's five in the morning – what d'you expect me to be wearing?"

"I've never cycled this early before," Jack whispered excitedly as they went through to the kitchen. "There are no cars."

"It's the best time of day," Twitch agreed. "I'm having a hot milk. Do you want one?"

Jack nodded, and Twitch poured two mugs of milk, added half a teaspoon of sugar to each and zapped them in the microwave. He motioned for Jack to follow him and they sat down on the back step.

"Listen."

Jack opened his eyes wide and stuck his head forward.

"Not like that. Relax. Close your eyes. Really listen."

Jack closed his eyes then immediately opened them and looked at the sky. "It sounds like there's hundreds of birds, but I can't see any."

Twitch took a sip of the sweet warm milk and said nothing.

Jack sat silently for a bit, listening. He drained his mug and put it down. He glanced at Twitch. "It's a lot of twittering. It's nice, I guess."

"This is my favourite sound. It's like having an invisible orchestra in your back garden. You can either take in the whole sound or focus on one instrument."

"You can't pick out one bird in all that." Jack waved his arms.

"You can, when you've learned how to listen. Each bird has a unique call, but you're hearing them all jumbled up together. Can you hear that high *peep-peep-peep* and then a trill?" He held up his finger. "There it is. Did you hear the trill?"

"I heard it," Jack whispered.

"Try and tune into that one song. There. *Peep-peep-peep-peep*, the trill. And again."

"I hear it!"

"That's a wren; they're tiny but loud."

"A wren." Jack nodded.

"Now, see if you can hear the call that's most like a tune you could whistle. Lower and less frantic than the wren's, more like a flute. It's the kind of tune a cheerful chap strolling down the road might whistle… There it is." Twitch whistled a repeat of the tune. "Do you hear it?"

Jack closed his eyes and his head moved as he tried to locate the sound. He stiffened and whispered, "I think I hear it."

"That's a blackbird. Now open your eyes and check out that sunrise." Twitch drained the last of his hot milk. "Best bit of the day."

The two boys sat in silence, looking and listening. Twitch stole a glance at Jack's face, his caramel-coloured flick just a matted fringe without hair product.

"Why are you here, Jack?"

"Just curious, I guess." Jack didn't look at him.

"Nobody gets up before five in the morning to return the bike of someone they bully and listen to birdsong, because they're curious."

"I told you. I'm not going to be a bully any more. I'm trying to make it up to you."

"And..." Twitch could tell there was something Jack wasn't saying.

"And ... Madden lives on my street. I don't want to bump into him." He stared at his hands and whispered, "I'm scared of him."

"You came over here to escape Peaky and Madden?"

Jack nodded. "You're the only person I know who isn't afraid of them." He looked out over Twitch's garden. "That's one of the things that drove me nuts about you. I was really mean to you, but you were never scared."

"I hated you," Twitch said, matter-of-factly.

"But you weren't scared?"

"Bullies care too much about what other people think of them." Twitch grinned at Jack. "They're weak."

"Hey!" Jack playfully punched his arm and laughed. "But I was curious about the dawn chorus. Do you do this every day?"

Twitch shook his head. "It's too cold in winter and not many birds singing. Spring's the best time of year to listen, when all the birds are calling for mates. Most of the birds singing are boys. I kind of like to think of them as my gang." He felt a sudden flare of self-consciousness heat his cheeks and dipped his head so that his fringe fell over his blinking eyes. "Silly, I know."

"No. I get it." Jack said. "It's a nice feeling, being part of a gang. Although, you know, Twitch, it's nicer if they're humans."

Twitch laughed and got to his feet. "I wouldn't know."

"Are you taking your pigeons out again today?" Jack asked, standing too.

Twitch nodded. "I think I should release Frazzle closer to home, but I want to try taking Squeaker further away."

"I could help you," Jack offered, following him back into the kitchen. "If you wanted, that is."

Twitch narrowed his eyes. "Sure. Why not?" He opened the cereal cupboard. "You hungry?"

The boys ate breakfast, fed the chickens, topped up the teapot bird bath and feeding stations on the lilac tree, then tidied the kitchen. Jack did everything Twitch asked him to without complaint.

"You know all about me now," Twitch said. "You've seen my house, my birds, but I don't know you at all."

"What do you want to know?"

"I don't know. What football team do you support? What stuff do you like? What makes you tick?"

"I support Arsenal, but only 'cause my dad does. I like watching scary movies and playing video games." Jack looked uncomfortable.

"What's wrong?"

"Well, I'm worried that I'm a bit … you know, boring, ordinary."

Twitch laughed and gave him a shove. "We should make sandwiches to take with us."

"Actually, I brought a lunch big enough for the both of us."

Twitch was taken aback. "How did you know I'd let you come with me?"

"I was going to follow you until you gave in," Jack admitted. "I also brought—" He stopped as Twitch's mum came into the kitchen.

"Good morning, Jack. This is a nice surprise." She looked at Twitch, blinking bleary eyes and smiling.

"Jack brought my bike back," Twitch explained. "He's going to come with me to take the squabs out for training."

"It helps if there's two of us," Jack said. "In case Frazzle flies off again."

"Well, isn't that nice?" Iris made herself a cup of tea and sat down at the table to drink it. "Twitch, I'm going to the supermarket this afternoon to do the weekly shop, so if you want anything special let me know."

Twitch shook his head.

"Right then, I'm going to have a relaxing Sunday morning and read the papers with my feet up."

"We're off to sort out the pigeons," Twitch said, ushering Jack out of the kitchen. As they left, Iris turned on the radio, and they heard the low mumble of a newsreader.

"What did you bring?" Twitch asked Jack in the hallway. "You said you'd brought something, just before Mum came in."

"Check this out," Jack said proudly, opening the front door. On the grass beside Twitch's bike was a small trailer and, inside it, a cage.

"Where did you get that?"

"I used to ride in it when I was little, on the back of my dad's bike. It hasn't been used for years, and the cage is from when our dog, Winnie, was a puppy. I know it's not a proper pigeon cage, but I felt bad about your basket getting crushed. These were in our garage. No one will miss them."

"We can put straw in the bottom of the cage," Twitch said, peering in, "and when the birds are inside, cover it with a blanket until we're ready to release them."

"And look." Jack lifted a carrier bag out of the trailer

and opened it to show Twitch packets of sandwiches, crisps, fruit drinks and sweets. "I bought these at the garage for our lunch."

"You've thought of everything," Twitch said, flattered that Jack had planned to spend the whole day with him. "Grab the cage and bring it up to the pigeon loft. I need to get dressed."

When Twitch clambered through the bathroom window, dressed in his camo shirt, combat trousers, and carrying a blanket to cover the cage, Jack was sitting watching Scabby pecking about looking for seed.

"I'm glad you stopped me from hurting him," Jack said, as Twitch lowered Squeaker and then Frazzle into the cage. "I'm sorry I ever did that."

"Yeah, well, he's all right now." Twitch gave him a half-smile. "I'm sorry I threw that stone at you."

Jack shrugged. "I deserved it."

"Let's forget it. Pretend it didn't happen."

"Really?" Jack looked hopeful and Twitch nodded.

"As long as you don't ever hurt another bird."

"I won't."

"Can you carry that cage down to the trailer without spooking the pigeons?"

"Yes, boss!" Jack sprang into action, whilst Twitch shut up the pigeon loft.

The pair set off for Aves Wood, Twitch cycling slowly with the two pigeons in the trailer behind him, Jack half running, half walking beside him, asking questions about where they were going to release the birds.

As Twitch pedalled, he glanced at Jack, still unsure whether he could trust him.

Suddenly Jack stopped dead, frozen like a statue. Twitch jammed on his brakes and looked over his shoulder. "What's the matter?"

"Do you hear that?" Jack stared at Twitch. "It's a blackbird, isn't it? It is, isn't it?"

Twitch chuckled and nodded. "Yeah, that's a blackbird."

Jack straightened up, looking delighted. "Blackbirds are brilliant."

For a split second, Twitch felt they connected, sharing a moment, and it alarmed him. He put his feet back on the pedals and pushed away. Jack jogged to catch up with him.

"Why are we going this way?" Jack asked.

"What do you mean?"

"I mean, why take the birds this way – to Aves Wood, if they might get lost in there? If we only need to go a mile away, why not go the other way to Plover Lock?"

"It doesn't matter which way we go. Pigeons can get lost anywhere, and this is the way I always go, to watch birds."

"Where do you watch them from?" Jack asked, a wily look on his face.

"Everywhere," Twitch replied, his guard immediately up. "There are two bird-viewing areas..."

"You're not the kind of person who sits on benches with picnicking families and points at robins." Jack cocked his head. "You're a loner, who seeks out rare birds."

"How do you know what I'm like?" Twitch pedalled a bit faster so that Jack had to sprint to keep up, and that made him out of breath, which stopped him from talking.

When they reached the car park for Aves Wood, Twitch stopped and Jack bent over, his hands on his knees, breathing deeply.

"I do know what a hide is," Jack gasped.

"I don't know what you mean."

"Your mum, last night. She asked if you'd shown me your hide. That's what is marked on your map, isn't it? You've got a secret den in Aves Wood for birdwatching, haven't you?"

Twitch stiffened. "And what if I have?"

"Don't panic." Jack waved a hand at him. "I'm fine with you not telling me where it is. It's just, on my way home last night, I got to thinking about you, your hide and your pigeons, and I wondered if you were planning to train them to take messages from your hide back to your house."

Twitch paused before giving the tiniest of nods.

"I knew it! That is *so cool*." Jack's eyes were shining. "Look, I get that you don't want me, of all people, muscling in and ruining things. But can I just say that if you wanted company, or someone to help you with the birds, or do anything at all" – he pointed to the cage and the trailer, his expression nakedly pleading – "I'd be really into helping. I'd even clean up the pigeon poo."

Twitch stared hard at Jack, looking for any flicker of insincerity or malice, but saw none. "Would you swear an oath never to reveal the location of the hide to any living soul, not even if they had you tied to a tree and were punching you?"

"I would," Jack replied, his expression serious.

"You understand that the hide is *my* place. You wouldn't be allowed to go there unless I said so."

"I understand."

Twitch ran his tongue over his teeth. "If you damaged the hide in any way, I would never forgive you."

"I know."

"OK." Twitch nodded. "Swear an oath then, and I'll take you there."

13

FOOTPRINTS IN THE SILT

The trailer wouldn't fit under the bracken cover, so Twitch carried the cage with Frazzle and Squeaker, and Jack dragged the trailer.

Jack seemed uneasy in the woods and kept glancing over his shoulder.

"It's early," Twitch said. "If you're worried about Peaky and Madden, don't be. The only people up are fishermen and joggers. Anyway, no one will find us where we're going. The police didn't even find my hide when they searched the woods."

Jack nodded but stayed silent as they made their way off the path and into the undergrowth. Twitch was taking him on a roundabout route to the hide, hoping to disorientate him so he couldn't return on his own.

"Put the trailer in there." Twitch pointed to a

thicket of bushes. "No one will see it. We'll get it on our way home."

As he waited for Jack to hide the trailer, he spotted a wisp of smoke through the trees, and moved towards it out of curiosity.

"Is your hide by the river?" Jack asked as they descended the bank.

"No, I just want to check something out." Twitch focused on the knotty tree roots so he didn't drop the cage. They reached the water's edge and he nodded upriver. "An abandoned campfire!" Putting the pigeon cage down, he looked around, but saw no one. They approached the heap of charred sticks with caution. Twitch squatted beside it, studying the ground.

"I wonder who made it," Jack mused. "Do you think it's been going all night?"

Twitch blew into the embers and the pile of ash glowed red. He nodded. "It's not gone out yet."

"Do you think it was Peaky and Madden?"

"No. There'd be litter, or beer bottles." Twitch considered the muddy silt. "Those are our footprints. The only other set are these." He pointed to the marks made by a pair of boots with patterned soles. "And look, this tree trunk has been rolled down the bank. It's what they sat on."

"One person, on their own, made this fire last night?" Jack looked scared, and Twitch felt goosebumps rising on his skin. They were both thinking the same thing. Was it Robber Ryan's fire?

"We've got to put it out," Twitch said, cupping his hands and dipping them in the icy river. He flung the water at the fire and it hissed at him. "We can't leave a fire burning in the woods." He kicked at the embers, spreading them, and dumped another handful of water on top. There was a sizzle, and Jack joined in. They poured water onto the wood until it was silent.

"If it was Ryan, he's gone now," Twitch said, to reassure himself as much as Jack. "And he picked a great spot. That tree over there, hanging out over the water – it's where I watch the kingfishers."

"There are kingfishers here?"

"Mmm-hmm." Twitch nodded. "This spring, I've seen three nesting couples. I'm not sure how many there are in total. It gets a bit confusing once the little ones fledge."

"I thought kingfishers lived in hot countries."

"You're confusing them with hummingbirds. Both move fast. The kingfisher is known as blue lightning, because that's what you see when it flies across the water. Hummingbirds are the only birds who can fly backwards."

"I'd love to see a kingfisher." Jack looked hopefully out at the gurgling river.

"Let's come back tomorrow morning," Twitch said, keen to get the pigeons to the hide. "We can look for them then." Picking up Frazzle and Squeaker's cage, he moved through the trees with renewed purpose, no longer choosing the winding paths. When the pond appeared in front of them, Twitch whispered, "Follow in my footsteps. The ground is treacherous here." He led Jack through the waterlogged land to the dense copse of trees. "This is it."

"What is?" Jack prodded the foliage, looking confused.

Twitch reached into the ferns and pulled the coat hanger, lifting the door flap.

"No way!" Jack looked astonished, then dropped to his knees and crawled in. Twitch was right behind him, pushing the cage through the door. Inside, Jack was gazing around in awe. "This place is unbelievable!"

"The back room is waterproof," Twitch said, a hint of pride in his voice.

Jack went and lay down in it, looking up at the ceiling lined with blue plastic.

Twitch took the blanket off the birdcage. Frazzle and Squeaker seemed unperturbed by their journey.

He thought about giving them some grain but remembered that it was better that they were hungry. "Do you want to help me take them up to the release platform?"

"Release platform?" Jack sat up.

"Yeah. This will be the first time I've used it." Twitch stepped up to the trunk of the beech tree. He untied two bits of string and pushed up the section of roof over the fire. "I made this hatch as a chimney, for the smoke to be drawn out of, but it is also a ladder." He reached through, jumping to grab the thick branch above the hole, and walked his feet up the tree trunk, climbing out of the hide. Sitting on the branch above, he looked down at Jack's eager face. "There's a stubby branch on the trunk to put your foot on. Follow me."

Twitch climbed higher with Jack right behind him. The trunk forked into three sturdy branches. In between them, Twitch had built a platform using a pallet that someone had dumped in the river. He'd measured the space, then cut the pallet to size with a hacksaw, winched it up into the tree, propped it on the three branches and wedged it into the intersection. It was just big enough for the two boys to sit cross-legged.

"Aren't you worried someone will see you up here?" Jack asked, looking around.

"No. I wear camouflage colours, sit still, and don't make a sound. Anyway, people never look up."

"I didn't realize there were special clothes for birdwatching." Jack peered down at his yellow T-shirt and faded jeans.

"You can get much closer to birds if you're quiet, move carefully and blend in with the plants."

"You make it sound like being a spy."

"You *are* spying, but on birds. Lots of them are shy or skittish around humans." He gave Jack a meaningful look. "With good reason."

Jack gazed up through the canopy to the sky. "Are you going to release the pigeons from here?"

"I was going to release Squeaker from here. Frazzle should probably be released closer to home. But, yeah, once they're used to the flight, I want to try strapping a message to their legs in tiny silver canisters."

"If you were at home, I could be here and send you a message."

"You don't know how to handle a pigeon." Twitch frowned. He'd not imagined anyone else being a part of his pigeon post, but it would be more fun if someone sent him a message, rather than sending messages to himself.

"You could teach me."

"We could try." They smiled at each other, then, suddenly self-conscious, turned to gaze out over the pond.

Twitch leaned forward as he spotted a dark figure amongst the trees. He grabbed Jack's arm. "Over there!" He pointed.

"Over where? What is it? A bird?" Jack eagerly scanned the water.

"No. A man. Wait here." Twitch scrambled off the platform and half climbed, half dropped down into the hide. He was back a minute later, binoculars around his neck. He handed them to Jack as he pulled himself onto the platform. "Round to the right of the pond," he gasped. "Take a look."

"Whoa, are these yours? They're cool." Jack put the glasses to his eyes. "I can't see anything."

"Move the dial between the lenses to focus them."

"Oh, I get it … hang on." After a long minute of peering through the binoculars, Jack lowered them, an unimpressed expression on his face. "It's just two girls and a blonde woman."

"You can't be looking in the right place," Twitch took the glasses and focused them on the spot where he'd seen the dark figure, but Jack was right. The only people he could see were a blonde woman in a pink anorak and, either side of her, Ava and Tippi, the girls who'd lied to him yesterday. He lowered the binoculars and frowned. "That's strange. They must have scared him away."

"Scared who away? Who did you see?"

"I saw a man with a shaved head in a long dark coat, like the picture in the newspaper," Twitch replied. "I think I saw Robber Ryan."

14

TWO BIRDERS IN A BUSH

"What should we do?" Jack looked at Twitch.

"I don't know." Twitch tucked his fringe behind his ear. "Do we tell the police? We don't know if it was actually him."

Jack shrugged. "We ought to. There's still officers patrolling the woods."

"All right, but let's release the pigeons first. Frazzle and Squeaker haven't eaten since yesterday. I'll climb down, get a rope, tie it to the cage and throw it up to you." He pointed. "Wrap the rope around that branch and then pull the cage up slowly. I'll climb beside it, making sure the birds aren't spooked."

Jack nodded and Twitch shinned down the tree as quickly as he could. He popped the lid off his buried plastic box and pulled out a length of rope. Jack winched the pigeon cage up and Twitch came with it. He had to sit on a branch, as there was no room for him on the platform.

"You know, we could fix the cage to the platform, give it a roof, camouflage it a bit, and it could be the hide pigeon loft," Jack suggested. It was a good idea, but Twitch felt funny about Jack having ideas concerning his birds and his hide.

Sensing he'd crossed a line, Jack went back to talking about the escaped robber. "Imagine if that *was* Ryan's fire that we put out."

"He could be hiding near by." Twitch gave an involuntary shudder.

"I wonder why the police haven't found him yet?"

"They didn't find my hide. Although it's impossible to see it from the paths. I made sure of that when I camouflaged it. And there's nothing in it that would interest sniffer dogs. Plus, the ground around here is waterlogged. When they did their big search, they probably went right round it. You can only see someone coming in or out of the hide if you are on the other side of the pond. So maybe they missed Ryan's hiding place too."

"What's on the other side of the pond?"

"There's only one path, and it's a dead end, totally overgrown. No one ever goes over there."

"Maybe that's where Ryan is hiding." Jack looked across the water. "Or where the loot is."

"Surely that's the first place the police would search?"

"Budge up a bit, so I can release Squeaker." Twitch shuffled around the tree.

"You know, if Frazzle gets lost again, I'll help you find him."

"You think I should release him too?"

"It's not up to me."

"It might be better to release them together. Then Frazzle can follow Squeaker." Twitch positioned himself beside the cage. "Right, you squabs," he said, encouragingly. "There's a mountain of grain in your pigeon loft. All you have to do is fly home and gobble it up." He opened the door, then looked at Jack. "Do you want to try picking up Squeaker?"

Jack's eyes grew wide and he nodded, shifting so he was the other side of the cage to Twitch. "What do I do?"

"Calmly, reach in with both hands and bring them together either side of her body, that's it, now gently bring them together. Yes." Jack gasped as he found he was holding Squeaker. "Keep your grip light, but firm, that's it and bring her out."

Twitch reached in and took hold of Frazzle. "On the

count of three, we'll release them together."

"Wait, how do I do that?" There was a note of panic in Jack's voice.

"Hold your arms out and open your hands. She'll do the rest." Twitch smiled encouragingly, but Jack hadn't taken his eyes off Squeaker. "Ready? One, two, three!"

Jack opened his hands and Squeaker leaped into the air, fanning out her wings with a clap. Frazzle chased his sister up through the canopy. They circled each other as they climbed, then both flew off in the same direction.

"I did it!" Jack was beaming. "I held a bird!"

"And if Frazzle follows Squeaker, I think he might actually make it home today." Twitch grinned. "But I won't count my chickens."

"You've got three."

"Ha ha, very funny." Twitch rolled his eyes. "Shall we go and find that police officer now?"

"Oh, yeah. We should," Jack said, searching the sky for the pigeons, but they were gone.

"We'll go out onto the main path," Twitch said as they climbed back down into the hide.

Leading Jack, Twitch went around the side of the copse of trees to the rabbit track that he'd followed on Friday evening when spying on Ava and Tippi.

"You really can't see it," Jack marvelled as he looked back over his shoulder at the hide. "It just looks like lots of nettles and brambles."

They tramped through the undergrowth until they reached the footpath. Twitch pointed. "Let's go this way. It'll take us to the main crossroads and the bridge over the river. There's bound to be a police officer there."

As the boys walked, Twitch listened for bird calls. "Tree sparrow." He heard it before he saw it. The tiny bird with a chocolate-brown cap and black bib was hopping from slender branch to slender branch, chirruping and cheeping.

"There's more than one kind of sparrow?"

"There are house sparrows, tree sparrows, rock sparrows and Spanish sparrows, but I've only seen the first two. The others live in warmer countries."

"So how do you know that's a tree one?"

"Its colours."

"It's brown."

"No, its belly is a beige-grey; you aren't looking closely enough."

"How are you meant to see? It hops about so quickly and then flies off."

"The more you look at the markings, the quicker you recognize the birds. You've spent time with Squeaker and Frazzle; tell me, what colour are their beaks?"

Jack stopped in his tracks, and Twitch thought he was going to answer, but instead he said, "Quick. Hide!" and jumped off the path, pushing through the ferns.

"What is it?" Twitch said, his heart jump-starting into a gallop.

Jack put his fingers to his lips and Twitch heard voices.

Terry and Vernon came walking along the path.

"This place is huge," Vernon complained.

"I know. That stolen money could be anywhere, and where is Jack?" Terry gabbled. "He might have already found it. Or given up. Or…"

"I say we go to the cafe and get chips," Vernon said.

"Good idea. Give us energy for digging. If the money is buried, that is. It might be in the river, or the pond…"

The boys' voices faded as they got further away. Jack popped his head out to check the coast was clear.

"Why did you do that?" Twitch asked.

"Do what?" Jack stepped out onto the path.

"Hide from Terry and Vernon."

"Well, you know…"

Twitch felt his spirits sink. "You didn't want them to see you hanging out with me, did you?"

"No. It wasn't that." Jack blushed. "Look, if we'd bumped into them, we'd have had to talk to them, and the last time—"

"Yeah. No. I get it." Twitch cut him off. He pushed his way back onto the path and stormed ahead of Jack, suddenly feeling very angry but not sure exactly why. Jack tried to catch up with him, which made him walk faster, and the two of them were almost running by the time they came to the crossroads where Constable Greenwood was standing talking to an elderly lady. Twitch knew the police officer because he delivered his Saturday paper.

"Hello, Twitch. Out for a spot of birdwatching?" Constable Greenwood greeted him.

"Constable Greenwood, we want to report something."

"We've seen Robber Ryan," Jack said.

"You've seen Ryan?" Constable Greenwood looked at Jack.

"Well, no. I haven't. Twitch has." Jack nudged Twitch.

"I'm not sure," Twitch admitted. "We've seen a few strange things and we thought we should report them in case it helps you find the escaped robber."

"Tell me what you've seen." Constable Greenwood took out a small notebook and pen, and Twitch told him about the campfire by the river, the footprints and the glimpse of a dark figure through the binoculars.

"That's very helpful," Constable Greenwood said, snapping his notebook shut. "Thank you."

"Don't you believe us?" Jack scrutinized the man.

"It's not a matter of believing you." Constable Greenwood smiled. "That lady I was talking to just now. She was telling me how Ryan followed her down the canal towpath this morning. I have to write down every reported sighting in my book, and they'll all be considered by the detectives in charge of the case, but there are some folk with overactive imaginations."

"But what about the fire?" Twitch said.

"Won't be the first fire someone's built by that river. I've known fishermen with a good catch make a little fire and cook themselves a fish for breakfast."

"Oh, right. Yeah. I didn't think of that." Twitch felt deflated.

"You mustn't worry, boys. We've got this investigation in hand."

Jack and Twitch shuffled away up the path in silence.

"Shall we go back to yours?" Jack suggested tentatively. "See if the pigeons made it back?"

"They either will or they won't," Twitch replied

blankly, still smarting at Jack making him hide from Terry and Vernon. "Once a bird's up in the sky, there's no knowing what's happening. I'll check on them this afternoon."

"Twitch, look, I wasn't embarrassed about being seen with you. That's not why…"

Twitch glared at Jack. "I never said you were."

"I'm sorry," Jack offered.

"I'm going back to the hide. I came here to watch birds," Twitch said. "You can do whatever you like."

"I want to watch birds too," Jack said meekly, following him.

Twitch nodded but said nothing more as he led the way back. Once they were through the door, Twitch kneeled and brushed the soil aside, lifting out the storage box.

"What's in there?"

"My birdwatching kit," Twitch replied, taking out the cushion and blanket. "Insect repellent." He sprayed some onto his hands and rubbed it all over his face and neck. "Want some?"

Jack shook his head. "What's that?"

"An Ordnance Survey map of the area." Twitch lifted it out. "That's an army rain poncho, and that's a pair of waterproof trousers."

"What are these?" Jack lifted out a handful of tiny silver canisters on Velcro straps.

"They're the messenger cylinders, for strapping to the pigeons' legs. You roll the message up and put it in the canister, then attach it to the bird's leg."

Jack unscrewed one and peered inside. "Do you sleep out here sometimes?"

"I haven't yet. I'm hoping to camp out this summer."

"When?"

"Don't know. When Mum lets me. Probably have to be after they've caught Ryan."

"I could camp out with you, if you liked." Twitch gave Jack a sideways look. "You wouldn't have to wait for permission then. You could tell your mum that you've been invited over to mine, and I'd tell my mum I'm sleeping at yours, and then we could come here." He smiled brightly.

"I don't lie to my mum."

"No, right, of course. Neither do I." Jack sighed. "Look, I didn't mean to ruin everything. I didn't want Terry and Vernon to see me because I forgot to tell them that the hunt for the cash was off, and … and … well, we were having a good time and I didn't want them to ruin it."

Twitch blinked, unsure whether to believe him.

"It would be fun to camp out here. The two of us. Don't you think?"

"We could cook baked potatoes and spaghetti hoops on the fire," Twitch said, remembering a time when his grandad had made the best-tasting dinner of his life. "And watch for nocturnal birds."

"Yeah, and toast marshmallows on sticks and tell spooky stories."

They smiled at each other.

"If you're going to become a birder, you'll need one of these." Twitch passed him a well-thumbed book with splayed pages. "It's a field guide of the birds in the UK and Europe."

"Is a birder a birdwatcher?"

"Yeah, a serious birdwatcher. Someone who knows how to ID birds, and the good places to see birds. They would have a list."

"A list?"

"Serious birdwatchers keep a list of all the species they've spotted. They get a thrill from seeing a lifer."

"What's a lifer?"

"A bird you haven't seen in your life that you want to add to your list."

"And what do you call a serious birdwatcher who keeps lists and goes after lifers?"

"A twitcher."

Jack stared at him, trying hard not to smile, but the corners of his mouth gave him away. "No way. A *twitcher*?" Twitch felt himself go red. "And you, you have a list, right?"

Twitch pulled his field journal from his pocket and Jack laughed raucously.

"But I'm not a twitcher," Twitch protested. "You have to have money to travel the world following rare birds."

"But one day you will."

"I'm happy here, being a birder."

"So how do I become a birder, like you?"

"By watching birds," Twitch replied gruffly, but he was smiling as he pushed open the pond window. "I'll show you."

15

WHAT'S EATING GILBERT?

Putting the binoculars to his eyes, Twitch scanned the reeds around the pond.

"See anything?" Jack asked.

"You've got to be patient," Twitch said, glimpsing a flicker of orange and focusing the glasses.

"What is it?"

"An oystercatcher. No. Two oystercatchers, stalking about in the reeds. Here, look." Twitch handed Jack the binoculars. "Do you see them? Black heads and long orange beaks that they stab into the water, looking for food." Twitch heard a high piping cry. "Do you hear that? That's them."

Jack had gone rigid and was wobbling the glasses, trying to make sense of what he was seeing.

"Don't jam your face into the lenses; you won't see

147

anything. Rest the tops against your eyebrows. Give your eyes space."

"I see them!" Jack cried. "Oh! Is that...? They've got a baby! Look!" He handed the binoculars back to Twitch, looking delighted. "I saw an oystercatcher chick."

Twitch took a glimpse and, sure enough, following in the wake of its parents was a ball of brown fluff, mimicking the head-bobbing, though its black beak was too short to pull anything from the water. "Yup, that's an oystercatcher chick." He passed Jack the field guide so he could look the bird up. "Oystercatchers are waders and normally live on the coast, but they come inland during nesting season. They follow the river."

"How many do I have for my list now? I've got oystercatchers, tree sparrows, swallows, blackbirds..."

"Rock doves," Twitch added, and Jack laughed.

"How long is your list?"

"One hundred and twenty-seven," Twitch replied without hesitation.

"Wow! Really?"

"That's not very many. There are nearly ten thousand different kinds. But I've never been outside Briddvale. You need to travel if you're going to see a lot of birds."

"Where would you go if you could?" Jack asked. "To see birds, I mean."

"New Guinea. It's a big island north of Australia. It's famous for being the home of the birds of paradise. Alfred Russel Wallace – this famous biologist – said that the bird of paradise is 'one of the most beautiful and wonderful of living things'." He looked at Jack. "I'd love to see a real one, in the wild. That would be something."

"I really want to see those kingfishers tomorrow. They're a good bird to have on a list, aren't they? They're rare." Jack looked excited. "I wonder how many types of birds I'll have spotted by the end of the summer."

"At least fifty."

"Fifty!"

"Shh." Twitch cocked his head, listening. "I thought I heard voices." He crawled into the triangular room, opened the peephole and set his binoculars in it.

"Is there anyone there?" Jack whispered.

Forging a path through the nettles and thistles were Ava and Tippi. They looked in a hurry and were glancing about furtively, as if worrying about being seen. When they neared the footpath they broke into a run. Once they were on it they visibly relaxed and slowed to a walking pace.

"It's those two girls we saw with that blonde woman. Their names are Ava and Tippi."

"What are they doing deep in the woods?"

"I don't know, but I have something I want to return to them." Twitch pulled the silver kingfisher bracelet from his pocket. "Let's go after them."

They shut up the hide and hurried round to the rabbit track, breaking into a jog to catch up with the sisters.

"They're coming up to the kissing gate." Jack pointed when they reached the crossroads and Twitch saw the sisters take a right turn away from Siskin Lock.

"Looks like they're heading up the canal."

"C'mon" – Jack broke into a jog – "or we'll lose them." He raced after them and turned, disappearing from sight for a second.

"Aargh!" Jack ran back and grabbed Twitch's arm. "What's that? It's huge!"

A stick-limbed grey bird with knobbly legs, an impressively sharp yellow beak and a wispy plume of black feathers stood on the path blocking the way to the gate. It stared at Jack with a distinctly unimpressed expression on its face.

Twitch laughed. "How are you going to be a birder if you're scared of birds?"

"I'm not scared. It gave me a shock, that's all. Why's it staring at me? Shoo, birdie, shoo!" Jack waved his arms, but the bird didn't move. "What's wrong with it? It looks angry."

"That's Gilbert," Twitch said, nudging Jack forward. "He's harmless."

"Gilbert," Jack muttered, pushing back against Twitch, "doesn't look harmless to me. That's a big beak he's packing."

"He's a grey heron. He stalks up and down this section of the canal like he owns the place." Twitch nodded at the bird. "Don't you, Gilbert?"

The bird slowly turned his head away disdainfully.

"Is Gilbert his real name?"

Twitch lifted an eyebrow. "He's a bird, Jack. They don't have names. Gilbert is what I call him."

"Oh yeah, right." Jack nodded. "I knew that."

Twitch opened the gate and Gilbert stalked through it. Following the bird, Twitch craned his neck and saw Ava and Tippi a couple of hundred metres down the towpath. They ran up to a blue canal boat with the name *Kingfisher* painted on the side in a cheery red. Pots exploding with flowers sat on the roof. The girls hopped aboard and disappeared down into the cabin.

"Do you think they live on the boat?"

"They told me they're on holiday," Twitch said, marching towards it.

When they reached the barge, he leaned over and knocked on the cabin door. A woman with a tapestry scarf around her neck, trimmed with assorted feathers, popped her head out. Her freckled brown skin looked like polished leather and her tightly curled grey hair was scraped into a bun, speared by sticks with colourful beads dangling off them.

"Can I help you?" Her voice was low and melodic.

"Hi, my name's Twitch; this is Jack. We found this." He held up the bracelet. "I think it belongs to Ava or Tippi."

The woman smiled when he used their names. "Climb aboard." She ducked back into the cabin and called out, "Girls, we have visitors."

The two boys glanced at each other and followed her in. There were interesting things in every nook of the cabin. A wooden carving of a barn owl was perched on a shelf stacked with bulging sketchbooks, paintbrushes were suspended from ceiling hooks, and two stained-glass panels – one depicting a scene of a boat on a river, and the other a kingfisher skimming the water – dangled in front of a window.

"How long have you been moored here?" Jack asked as they gazed around.

"We arrived three days ago."

"Are you staying long?" Twitch asked, noting that Ava had lied to him.

"As long as it takes."

"As long as what takes?"

"As long as it takes to see the kingfishers."

"Is that why your daughters were visiting the nature reserve this morning?" Jack asked.

The shadow of a troubled expression crossed the woman's face and then was gone. "They are my *grand*daughters. And yes, they were looking for kingfishers."

"Twitch knows where the nests are," Jack said.

"Your boat ..." Twitch began.

"... is called the *Kingfisher*. Yes." She nodded. "I'm Nancy Kingfisher, but everyone calls me Nan; I'm an artist. This boat is my home. We came to Briddvale specifically to see the kingfishers. It's our family bird, but the girls have never seen one."

"Where do you normally live?" Jack asked.

"If you have a boat, you can call anywhere home," Nan replied.

"I can show you where the nests are," Twitch offered. "Do you have a map of Aves Wood?"

"I do, somewhere." Nan turned her back and riffled through a pile of papers.

"Oh! It's Gilbert." Twitch pointed at an easel standing in the dining area beyond the kitchenette.

"He calls the grey heron Gilbert," Jack explained. "They're old friends."

"Herons are supposed to be shy, but not Gilbert." Twitch studied the picture. "It looks just like him."

"I admire a bird that sticks around long enough for me to draw it. Ah, here it is. The nature reserve map."

Twitch took in the rows of jam jars stuffed with pens and pencils, charcoal, pastels and brushes that lined the window ledges, as he took the map from her. "You paint birds?"

"I draw from nature – plants, insects, birds, mammals – and sometimes I sell my pictures; but mostly I illustrate books."

"I'd like to live on a boat," Jack said wistfully.

"It is a life of adventure, blessed with still moments," Nan said, nodding.

Twitch sat down at the table and, picking up a pencil, marked the map with three crosses.

The door leading to the rest of the boat had been turned into a noticeboard by a covering of cork tiles. Scraps of drawings, torn-out pictures from magazines, postcards, notes in a spidery handwriting and photographs were pinned to it. The door opened. Tippi and Ava came in.

"Oh, it's you," Ava said, looking unimpressed.

"My name's Twitch," he said, ignoring her rudeness and smiling at Tippi.

"And I'm Jack," Jack added, blushing.

"Did you find your pet pigeon?" Tippi asked Twitch.

"Yes, we found him in the car park."

This made Tippi giggle.

"We saw you and your sister in the woods earlier," Jack said. "You were talking to a blonde woman."

Every muscle in Ava's body went rigid. "We didn't know her," she said sharply. "She was asking directions, but we couldn't help, because we don't live around here."

Tippi was nodding hard. Twitch peered through his fringe and saw Nan giving Ava a look with meaning. The silent communication of some instruction, but he didn't understand what it meant.

"Twitch is marking where the kingfisher nests are on the map," Nan said, changing the subject.

"Really?" Ava studied Twitch with sudden interest. "You know where they live?"

Twitch nodded. "They nest in the banks of the river" – he pointed to his crosses – "on this side, away from people." He looked down at the map. "To watch the birds, you need to be in one of three viewing spots. Here, here or here." He drew small circles. "And you need to be there early in the morning, when it's quiet. If you stand here, in the middle of Bridd Bridge, you'll see the birds rocketing up and down the river, kissing the water like a skimming stone."

"Did you know the kingfisher is known as blue lightning?" Jack said with authority.

"Everybody knows that," Tippi replied with a giggle.

"We came here to give you this." Twitch held up the bracelet. "You dropped it the other day."

"Oh, look, Ava!" Tippi clapped. "It's not lost after all. Thank you, Twitch. Ava loves that bracelet. I have one too. They were a present from—" Ava shut her up with a gentle kick to her ankle.

"Yes, thank you." Ava smiled at Twitch as she took the bracelet. "It's my favourite." She put it on her wrist and picked up the map. She stared at him blankly. "Thanks for coming."

"We should probably be going," Jack said, nudging Twitch. He looked at Nan. "Your boat is amazing. Thanks for inviting us in to see it."

They waved their goodbyes and sauntered back along the towpath.

"They were hiding something," Twitch said quietly. "When you said we'd seen the girls this morning, a funny look came over Nan's face. And Tippi was nodding like mad when we said we saw them with the blonde lady."

"I didn't notice that," Jack said, "but I did notice how pretty Ava is."

Twitch shook his head. "Did you see Ava kick Tippi to stop her telling us where the bracelet came from?"

Jack gave him an apologetic look. "My mum always says I'm not very observant."

"Some birdwatcher you're going to be." Twitch laughed. "I think those girls are hiding something."

"Maybe we should visit them again tomorrow?" Jack suggested.

Twitch eyed him suspiciously. "So you can flirt with Ava?"

"No." Jack grinned. "Maybe."

They returned to Aves Wood through the kissing gate and took the path that led to the rabbit trail, passing a pair of police officers stationed at the junction.

"Ryan's still at large," Twitch commented.

As they approached the trail, he pointed out a rusty old shopping trolley up in the branches of a tree. It had been there for so long the tree had grown around it.

"That's the marker for the path." He checked the coast was clear. "Be quiet, move fast, stay low," he ordered, before making a mad dash through the undergrowth. When they reached the hide, they scrambled inside, talking excitedly about eating their picnic lunch.

If either of them had turned back or glanced over his shoulder, he would have seen Ava and Tippi emerging from the bushes beside the hide.

16

GONE FISHING

The next morning, when Twitch arrived on the left bank of the River Bridd, where he'd agreed to meet Jack, it was gone six thirty. He'd already taken Frazzle and Squeaker, in their new cage, to the hide, climbed the tree and left them on the platform to get used to their second residence. Both pigeons had made it back to their loft yesterday and his confidence in their ability to find home was growing. He thought he and Jack might try strapping a message canister to Squeaker's leg today as she was more reliable than Frazzle.

"Twitch!"

Looking up, expecting to see Jack, Twitch was surprised to see Ozuru from school wearing waders and standing in the river. Ozuru hadn't spoken a word to him since he'd kicked him in the ribs in the fight over Scabby.

"Ozuru? What are you doing here?"

"Fishing with my dad." He pointed to a spot along the bank where there were two camping chairs and two rods set up. Ozuru's dad was studying the river, looking for the flicker of approaching fish. "You know, father and son time." Ozuru rolled his eyes. "Why are you out so early?"

"Oh, you know." Twitch blinked. "Birdwatching."

"Come to see the kingfishers?"

Twitch lifted his head, surprised. "Yeah."

"I've seen them. They've been fishing too. They're better at it than me. I've caught nothing." He glanced back at his dad, to check he wasn't being missed, then waded closer. "Listen. I…" He cleared his throat, looking uncomfortable. "I'm not good at fighting. I don't like it."

Twitch frowned, wondering what Ozuru was trying to say.

"I'm scared of being hit. I panic. I freeze." He seemed distressed, so Twitch nodded as if he understood. "That time, with the pigeon. I froze when you threw that stone at Jack and ran at Terry. Then Vernon picked you up and Jack was bleeding, and I was standing there doing nothing."

"You kicked me when I was down."

"I wouldn't have done it if you were up," Ozuru

160

said seriously. "You might have hit me. You could beat me in a fight, easy. I kicked you because I didn't want the others to know I was a coward." Ozuru looked ashamed.

"There's nothing cowardly about refusing to fight," Twitch said, repeating something his grandad used to tell him. "It takes courage to stand your ground." Ozuru blinked, thinking this through. "But you kicked me when the fight was over. That's the opposite of brave."

"I've felt bad about it ever since," Ozuru admitted. "I'm sorry. I wish I hadn't kicked you. I did it so the others would think I was like them." He shook his head. "I suck."

"Hey." Twitch gave him a half-smile. "It didn't hurt that much."

"It didn't?"

Twitch shook his head. "You come fishing often?"

"My dad started bringing me last year. I really like it." His face lit up. "It's peaceful. The sound of the water is relaxing. And it feels amazing when you catch a fish and see it up close. But the best bit is putting them back in the river and seeing them swim away." His expression changed. "You won't tell anyone, will you?"

"What's wrong with liking fishing?"

"It's not cool." Ozuru looked concerned. "I pretend

my dad forces me to come, but really it's the other way around."

"Your secret is safe with me." Twitch chuckled. "I'm a birder, after all."

"Thanks." Ozuru gave him a bashful smile.

"Your dad wants you…" Twitch pointed to Ozuru's father, who was gesticulating at his son to get out of the river and stop scaring all the fish away.

"I'd better go." Ozuru shrugged. "I really am sorry for kicking you, Twitch."

Twitch nodded and watched him splash away. He glanced at his watch. It was five to seven; Jack should be arriving any minute. He headed up towards the path and heard the rhythmic *thud, thud, thud* of running feet.

"Billy!"

"Twitch!" Billy came to a stop. "You startled me."

Dressed in jogging bottoms, a vest and a baseball cap, Billy's muscly tattooed arms were shiny with sweat. He looked like a boxer in training.

"Sorry. You out for a jog?"

"No, I'm shopping for a dress! Yes, of course I'm out for a jog. Got to keep fit, or I'll end up with a belly like me da's." He lifted his vest and slapped his stomach, which was an intimidating washboard of abdominal muscles.

"I don't suppose you've seen Jack, have you?"

"The boy who likes to feed you worms? No." Billy looked over his shoulder. "Are you hiding from him? Want me to knock him over for you? I could trip him, make it look like an accident."

"No!" Twitch said, horrified. "We're friends now."

"Really?" Billy arched an eyebrow.

"We're meeting here to see the kingfishers."

"Kingfishers?" Billy straightened up. "The birds?"

"Yes, there are some nesting in the riverbank. Aves Wood is famous for them."

"Is it now?" Billy seemed amused. He leaned against a tree and studied Twitch. "Listen, Twitch, about Jack. A leopard doesn't change his spots, you know?" He fixed him with a meaningful look. "You should be careful."

"Jack's all right."

"You're sure about that, are you?"

As Billy watched him, Twitch realized he wasn't entirely sure about Jack yet. He'd enjoyed their time together yesterday, and Jack seemed to like looking at birds, but then he remembered hiding from Vernon and Terry.

"You might know a lot about birds, kiddo, but you don't seem to know a lot about people."

"Birds are more straightforward than people."

"You're not wrong." Billy nodded. "Ask yourself this: what happens when you go back to school? Will Jack be your friend then?"

"I don't know," Twitch admitted.

"Then ask him. Now, I've something to ask you." Billy pointed across the river to the opposite bank. "What's over there?"

"Nothing much. The embankment up to the railway line, which is too steep to climb. If you cross the bridge and follow the path, there's good dragonfly-and-damselfly spotting by the ponds. Beyond that is Tag Cut, the water cut-through the old barges used to cross the river and get to the power station. It's tough to walk because the path's overgrown with Japanese knotweed. It's a dead end, so no one really goes there."

"But you can get there?"

"If you really want to. I've been a couple of times, to see what's nesting. Found nothing but bramble scratches and nettle stings." Twitch followed Billy's gaze. "Why?"

"Oh, nothing. I was just wondering if it was worth taking a look. Obviously it isn't." Billy smiled broadly. "I should get on. Come see the van later, if you like." He jogged on the spot. "I'll be there all afternoon." And then he was off.

Twitch sat down to wait for Jack, thinking about what Billy had said. He looked across the river, wondering what Billy had seen there to make him curious. Twitch wanted to like Billy; the man was always kind to him, but he acted shifty, and that bothered him.

After waiting half an hour, Twitch grew restless. Jack was late and Twitch wasn't sure what he should do. Perhaps he'd got the meeting place wrong or run into Peaky and Madden. He decided to go back to the hide and check Jack wasn't waiting there, then do a circuit of the reserve.

There was no sign of Jack at the hide, so Twitch made for the east gate, the one closest to Jack's house. Walking quickly and quietly, Twitch passed dog walkers and anglers but there was no sign of Jack.

"What are you doing here?"

Twitch spun round to find Ava and Tippi were right behind him.

Tippi giggled. "We scared you."

"No, I … I'm looking for Jack."

"He's down by the rope swing near the bridge," Ava told him.

"He is?"

"Yeah, with two boys. They were fooling about, chucking rocks into the water."

"Two boys?"

"A skinny boy with dark curly hair, and a really big guy."

Twitch felt his stomach drop. Jack was with Terry and Vernon.

"What's the matter?" Ava asked.

"Those boys don't really like me," Twitch confessed. "They're kind of bullies."

"Then they're idiots." Ava's eyes blazed. "And Jack's an idiot too, for hanging out with them." Twitch was taken aback by her anger. "Sorry, it's just I hate bullies. I get bullied a lot at school. You're nice. You're better off without him."

"Thanks," Twitch said, sweeping his fringe away from his eyes. "Are you going to look for kingfishers? I could show you where the nests are if you like."

"No, we're—" Tippi started to speak, but Ava cut her off.

"We're going to feed the *ducks*." She gave her sister an anxious look.

"Duckies!" Tippi said and quacked enthusiastically.

"So, we'll see you around," Ava said.

"Oh, right. Yeah. See you." Twitch headed off down the path away from the bridge, but once he was out of sight, he doubled back and made his way towards it, through the trees. He was hoping Ava was wrong about Jack. But if she was right, he wanted to see for himself.

The path that led to the bridge had an offshoot that looped around to the riverbank. Years ago someone had tied a rope around a log and secured it to an overhanging tree branch, creating "the swing". Kids loved to dangle over the water and often ended up getting wet, but Twitch had never really used it, because you needed someone to push you and he usually came to the woods on his own.

As he approached, Twitch heard voices and laughter. He didn't take the offshoot path but carried on to the bridge. From the high vantage point overlooking the water, he peered down unobserved through the thick iron mesh fence and saw Terry wrestling with Vernon, trying to force him into the river. Vernon was too heavy and too strong, and he laughed as Terry struggled and grunted. Someone threw a big stone and splashed both of them. Ozuru emerged from under the bridge, no longer clad in wading trousers.

"I don't get it." Ozuru sounded puzzled. "What's so bad about liking birds?"

"I love birds," Vernon said, looking over. "Roasted, with chips."

Twitch knew immediately they were talking about

him. He put his face to the mesh to see better.

"He's a bit … you know." Terry shrugged. "Odd. I mean, he picked a pigeon over Jack. And don't forget" – he turned his head and looked at someone Twitch couldn't see – "he cut your face."

"It didn't hurt." Jack stepped out from the shadow of the bridge, legs astride, hands on his hips, yellow cap on backwards like some modern-day Peter Pan, and a wave of betrayal crashed over Twitch.

Vernon crowed like a cockerel and chased after Terry, clucking and calling, "Friend! *Bwark-bwark*, Twitch friend!"

Twitch heard Jack laughing and he clenched his teeth, stepping backwards. He didn't want to see any more. Jack had stood him up, left him waiting around like a pathetic idiot. Billy's words sounded in his head.

"You might know a lot about birds, kiddo, but you don't seem to know a lot about people."

"He has a pet chicken called Eggbum," Jack said, and the boys all roared with laughter as Twitch pivoted and ran.

BE MORE GOOSE

Before Twitch could think straight, he was crawling back through the door of his hide, angry and hurt. He tried watching the birds in the pond, but he couldn't calm down enough to sit still. He kept thinking about Jack's behaviour the previous day, turning up at five in the morning with the trailer and cage. Had it all been fake? Had he pretended to want to be Twitch's friend as some kind of dumb revenge for the stone that had cut his precious face?

Most of all, Twitch was furious with himself. Jack had proved repeatedly over the past few months that he hated him, and yet he'd let Jack into his home, shown him his birds, told him his secrets and even brought him to his hide. He was an idiot and Billy was right. Leopards didn't change their spots and he didn't understand people at all.

Throwing himself down onto the blue crate, Twitch thought about the Irishman who'd appeared like a knight in shining armour when Jack had been trying to shove a worm into his mouth. Billy had secrets, Twitch was sure of it, but he'd recognized Jack for what he was: a bully who couldn't be trusted. Twitch suddenly remembered that he'd stashed the Fruit Gums Billy had bought him at the bottom of his storage box, and he kneeled to dig them out. The sugary sweets instantly made him feel better. He thought about Billy's invitation to check out his camper van and decided that would be more fun than sitting here in the hide waiting for Jack to bring Vernon along to smash it up. He hoped Billy wouldn't mind him turning up a bit earlier than his invitation.

The path along the bottom field of Mr Patchem's farm had been baked to cracking point; the earth ripped apart by the heat. The buzzing of insects in the hedgerow seemed to be tuned into the frequency of Twitch's anger. He picked up a stick and whacked at drooping nettles, decapitating them while fantasizing about pushing Jack in the pond.

The orange and white VW camper van was in the far corner of the next field, half hidden in the shadow of a great oak. Twitch ducked down behind the hedgerow, suddenly aware that what he was about to do might be a bad idea. His mum had told him a million times not to trust strangers, and even though Billy had been nice to him, Twitch didn't know anything about the man or what he was really doing in Briddvale. Pushing aside a handful of branches, Twitch peered up the fallow field and saw Billy beside his van, lifting a kettlebell weight, doing reps. Twitch watched as Billy lunged and lifted over and over again; he was very strong.

Suddenly a thought popped into Twitch's head that made sense of this super-strong, super-secretive man who'd appeared a few days ago. What if Billy was an undercover police officer, working on the Robber Ryan case?

Twitch turned this idea over in his head as he watched Billy put the weight down and begin shadow-boxing. He looked like he could be a policeman. Standing up, Twitch walked slowly across the middle of the field, so Billy would see him coming.

"Hello," he called out as he approached.

Billy looked up and smiled, grabbing a towel from the bonnet of the van and wiping his face. "Twitch! You came sooner than I expected. Your plans change?"

Twitch nodded. "You were right about Jack."

"I'd better put the kettle on then, or would you rather have something cold?"

"Do you have a stove in the van?" Twitch asked, curious about how the inside was kitted out. He'd always thought it must be so cool to have a van you could live in.

"Sure do." Billy smiled. "Would you like to make the tea?"

Twitch followed him round the back of the van, his senses alert in case Billy turned into one of those dangerous strangers his mum went on about. A canvas canopy stretched out from the roof making a patch of shade, and the central door was wide open, so he could see the miniature kitchen. "That's so cool."

Billy gestured. "The matches are by the stove top, kettle's there, water's in the tap. Knock yourself out."

Twitch cautiously stepped inside, putting the kettle on and exploring the cupboards, finding two plates, two cups, two glasses, two pans and some tins of food. He looked around, hoping to see clues that would give away something about Billy's life, but there were no knick-knacks, photos or homely things like Nan had on her boat, just a suitcase unzipped on the passenger seat, a stew of clothes inside it.

"Is this *your* van?" Twitch asked Billy, who'd moved a folding chair to a spot in the sun.

"Course. Who else's would it be?" Billy sat down and closed his eyes.

The kettle began to whistle, and Twitch turned off the gas.

"Milk's in the fridge," Billy called out, eyes still closed.

"Thought it might be rented."

"Why?"

"You don't have much stuff."

"Sorry to disappoint you," Billy chuckled, "but I live in a house, like most people. This is my holiday accommodation, and sometimes, when it rains, or if I need a bath" – he shaded his eyes with his hand and looked at Twitch – "I stay in hotels."

Twitch carried the two cups of tea outside and set them on the camping table. "Are you a twitcher?"

"Beg your pardon?"

"Do you drive around looking for rare birds?"

"You could say that. I've come to Aves Wood to find kingfishers."

Twitch frowned. "But you didn't know Aves Wood had kingfishers until I told you about them this morning."

"That's right, and now that I do know, that's why I'm here. Life's funny like that. Sometimes you only find out why you're doing something after you've done it." Billy sat up. "Why don't you tell me about this Jack feller. What's his beef with you?"

Twitch told the story of how he'd saved Scabby but made an enemy out of Jack, and then how he'd saved Jack from Peaky and Madden, and thought they were becoming friends, until Jack had stood him up and then he'd overheard Jack and the other boys mocking him.

"Ditch him," Billy said, with a nod of the head.

"What?"

"He's not your friend. He's your enemy. Ditch him."

Twitch blew the steam from his cup of tea and, hearing the soft applause of wing flaps, looked up as a flock of Canada geese flew low over the field in a V formation, all seven of them landing simultaneously on the grass.

"Lovely landing, lads!" Billy called out and Twitch laughed. "My da told me, Canada geese are a feral species. They were brought here, like the grey squirrel. Now there's nearly more geese than pigeons. They've adapted to live alongside us, which annoys my da intensely. They don't even bother to migrate any more."

He pointed. "Bet you any money those geese have never seen Canada."

"Pigeons are nicer than geese. With geese, you never know if they're going to lose their temper."

"Maybe that's what you need to do, Twitch. Lose your temper. Be more goose. Adapt." Billy looked at him. "Grow a thicker skin. Accept that most people will disappoint you." He grinned. "Then it'll be a nice surprise when someone doesn't."

"My grandad used to say that you should always try and see the positive in everything and everyone."

"Well, there's nothing positive about me." Billy winked. "I'm a rotten human being."

Twitch laughed.

"You always been into birds?" asked Billy.

"Since I can remember. My grandad used to take me birding when I was little. We'd pack a tent and camp, so we could watch for night birds. I still use his binoculars."

"You miss him." Billy nodded and Twitch found he was nodding too. "My da had this saying that's always seemed true to me." He looked out over the field. "He'd say, 'Son, life is like licking honey from a briar', and he was right."

They watched the geese waddling across the field, dipping their beaks into the long grass.

"What do you do?" Twitch asked. "For a job, I mean, when you're not driving around in a camper van."

Billy paused. "I'm a teacher."

"What do you teach?" Twitch asked, pretty certain this wasn't true.

"Geography."

"I wish you were my geography teacher. My teacher, Mr Smelting, is a sour old duffer who can make anything boring."

Billy laughed.

"Do you live in Ireland?"

"No, no, I don't, Sherlock Holmes. I live in England. I start teaching at a new school in September, so I'm between places right now. All my stuff is in storage." Billy shifted in his seat, uncomfortable at being interrogated, and he changed the subject. "Listen, Twitch, about this Jack feller. Don't take it too personally. You need to realize it's a dog-eat-dog world. If you're not at the top of the pecking order, you're at the bottom."

"But what about friendship? Doesn't that count for anything?"

Billy shrugged. "Jack's doing what he needs to, to stay on top. That's obviously more important to him than friendship."

"He's an idiot. I hate him," Twitch said passionately. "He and the other boys are probably at my hide, smashing it up and laughing at me." He gritted his teeth. "He swore he'd keep it a secret."

"You have a hide?"

"On the near side of the pond. Last summer, I built a camouflaged den there because that's where all the best birds are. At the feeding tables you only get sparrows, nuthatches and tits. And it's really good. I mean, it's so well hidden that the police didn't even find it when they searched the woods," he boasted. "I was going to spend the summer birdwatching, then that stupid robber escaped, and now the reserve is full of people and police officers, and then Jack pretended to be nice…"

"The police never found your hide?"

Twitch shook his head. "It's off the paths, in the middle of a bunch of trees. I planted brambles and nettles all around it."

Billy's eyebrows rose. "That's impressive. I'd love to see it. You know, if Jack hasn't already trashed it."

"Really?"

"Really." Billy nodded, tossing the dregs of tea from his mug into the long grass. "I could swing by this afternoon, bring the camera, you know, in case there are any good pond birds to snap."

"Oh, there are. There's a family of oystercatchers with a baby chick."

"Cool. I love oystercatchers. Shall we meet at Bridd Bridge, say, three o'clock?"

"Yeah, OK." Twitch smiled, picturing Jack's face as he turned up at the hide with Vernon, only to find Billy there. He stood up. "I should go, but I'll see you at three."

18

PIGEON POST

Billy's words fluttered about Twitch's head. As he walked back to Aves Wood, his anger subsided. He didn't need Jack. He had always known that popular kids didn't befriend boys like him. It went against the natural order of things. He had managed fine without Jack before and he would do again. He'd adapt.

Collecting his bike from underneath its bracken blanket, Twitch lifted it over the kissing gate and wheeled it along the towpath back towards home. The sun was warm on his face and a drowsy bumblebee buzzed as it landed its fuzzy body on the purple head of a bending thistle.

A bright song in the hedgerow stopped him. *"Cheep-chap-chip-chap-chip-chap-chup-chap."* Perching on a thorny branch was a delicate olive-brown bird as small as a blue tit, with a hint of yellow trim to its feathers.

"I know who you are, little chiffchaff," Twitch whispered. "You don't need to sing your name at me." The bird turned its head, a pale brow and dark eye-stripe making it appear pretty. "You needn't worry about me; I'm fine. I'm going to toughen up." As if satisfied by his reply, the chiffchaff flitted away.

Dropping his bike on the grass in his front garden, Twitch let himself into the house. It was Monday lunchtime. Mum was at work. He went through the kitchen out into the garden and opened the box beside the back door where he kept the bird food. Pulling out bags of seed, peanuts and suet balls, he carried them to the teapot tree, unhooking the dangling feeders first and topping them up, before getting the stepladder and filling up the teapot feeders.

Feeding the birds always calmed him; he enjoyed the excited chirruping and fluttering of feathers around the feeders once they were full. Some peanuts fell on the grass and a magpie swooped down, hopping over to scoop one up in its beak. Twitch saluted the black and white bird, out of habit more than superstition, although he admitted to himself that he was feeling pretty sorrowful. There was a noisy battering of feathers and he almost rocked over the ladder as he twisted to see five more magpies descend from the skies, immediately squabbling and tussling over the nuts. He threw down more, and once they each had a nutty nugget in their beaks the birds flew away.

Six! Six magpies, he thought, reciting the old rhyme out loud: "'One for sorrow, two for joy, three for a girl, four for a boy. Five for silver, six for gold, seven for a secret never to be told.'

"Hey, girls," Twitch called to the chickens as he descended the steps. "It's going to be me that finds Ryan's money. The magpies say so. It's destiny."

Eggbum strutted up to him as he opened the gate to the chicken run and he greeted her with a hug, picking her up in his arms, loving her all the more because Jack had been mean about her name. Putting her down as he neared the coop, Twitch reached up to the shelf above the nesting boxes, which contained three circular biscuit tins with punctured lids, and lifted down the nearest one. He thought how good it would be if he did find the missing loot and how sorry Jack would be for betraying him. He prised the lid off the biscuit tin. In it was a mixture of bran, a piece of bread and chunks of carrot, and squirming amongst it all were mealworms. The birds loved them. He used to buy mealworms from the pet store, but they were expensive, and so he'd learned how to breed them in a larvae farm.

He sifted his fingers through the bran, and a couple of adult darkling beetles scurried away from him as he lifted his hand, palm piled with wriggling mealworms, which he tipped into the lid. When he had a good plateful, he carried them over to the chickens' food trough and dropped them in. Eggbum ran over, immediately filling her beak. Fandango danced across a moment later and Dodo squawked with outrage that she was the last to the dinner trough.

Amita's head popped up over the wall separating their gardens. "Ah, Twitch, you're just the person I was looking for. Tomorrow I wish to harvest the vegetables and fruit from my allotment, and I am looking for a strong young man to help me. Payment is very good." She held up a hand and counted off on her fingers. "A basket of courgettes, plenty of tomatoes, green beans, and as many raspberries as he can eat on the job." She looked at him questioningly. "Do you know any strong young men who might be interested in such well-paid work?"

Twitch smiled. "I'll do it, Amita."

"Wonderful, wonderful. Be ready at eight o'clock sharp."

"I will."

"Thank you, Twitch. You're a good boy."

Looking up at the pigeon loft, Twitch realized with a jolt that he'd forgotten Frazzle and Squeaker. They were still in their cage up the tree at the hide! He'd been so caught up in his own feelings that he'd forgotten the birds. They would be hungry, and if Jack had taken the others to the hide, possibly frightened. He needed to take them some food. He hurried through the house and climbed out of the bathroom window. He filled a sandwich bag with grain to take to the hide, then opened the wardrobe door to top up Scabby and Maude's bowl, but was stunned to find all four pigeons inside.

Frazzle was stuffing his face with birdseed and Squeaker had a tiny silver canister attached to her leg. Twitch reached in and unfastened the Velcro strap, staring uncomprehendingly down at the shining capsule in the palm of his hand.

Jack had released the birds!

It was like being punched in the stomach. He could barely breathe.

Not only had Jack released the birds, but he'd managed to attach a message to Squeaker's leg. That meant he had definitely been in the hide and he'd sworn not to do that. Twitch had all the evidence of betrayal he needed.

An image of Jack showing the hide to Vernon, Ozuru and Terry popped into Twitch's head. Jack pretending he'd built it all by himself. The boys lighting a fire and toasting marshmallows, laughing and talking about how stupid Twitch was. It was worse than them smashing the place. He cursed himself for being nice to Ozuru this morning.

Bristling with anger, Twitch felt his pulse throbbing in his temples and his head ached. With trembling hands, he unscrewed the top of the silver canister and pulled out a rolled-up strip of paper. He started to unfurl it, but seeing Jack's handwriting made him furious and he scrunched it up in his fist. He didn't need to read the message. He knew it would be one of three things, a taunt, a lie or a trap, and he wasn't going to fall for Jack's tricks any more. He stuffed the paper in his pocket, filled the pigeons' food and water bowls and slammed the wardrobe door shut, making Maude and Frazzle flutter off their perches.

He clambered back into the bathroom and washed his hands angrily, scrubbing at his skin with a nail brush.

He couldn't understand why he was so upset. A week ago he'd had no real friends to speak of. Today was no different from last Monday. But Jack's friendliness had changed everything. It had felt nice sharing things with someone, and it felt horrible to realize that Jack's friendship had been a mean trick. Well, Twitch was going to adapt, like the geese. He would find a new spot and build a new hide, one that he'd never share with anyone, ever.

He wondered what state the hide would be in when he met Billy at three o'clock. Jack might still be there. He pictured himself turning up with Billy, and smiled as he imagined Jack, Vernon and Terry running away as the strong man chased them into the pond, threatening to beat them up.

19
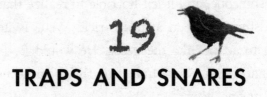

TRAPS AND SNARES

Billy was waiting for him at the bridge at three o'clock, unlike Jack, who hadn't shown up at all.

"Lead on, young man." Billy said cheerily. "You're the boss."

"Follow me."

"I'm looking forward to seeing this hide."

"If Jack hasn't trashed it."

"Well, if Jack has trashed it, we'll trash him."

Twitch felt important as he led Billy through the reserve. He pointed out the tree with the rusted shopping trolley wedged in its branches that was the secret marker of when to step off the footpath. They took the rabbit trail towards the pond, and as they crossed the soggy ground, Twitch pointed out the areas that were firm and the danger spots where the earth dissolved into invisible puddles.

Billy was glancing about keenly. "Have the police not searched this area for Ryan?"

"Oh, yes, they have. They even went out on the pond in boats, and poked about in the reeds with long sticks, but they didn't find anything, or anyone. No one could hide out here for very long without falling into the water, unless they knew the place really well."

Billy glanced sideways at him. "Where's this hide of yours, then?"

"Over there." Twitch pointed, relieved to see that, from the outside at least, it didn't look like it had been damaged.

Billy's brow furrowed as he studied the trees. "I can't see it."

Twitch smiled. "Neither can the birds."

The door to the hide was closed and there was no sign of movement within. Twitch felt a ripple of disappointment that his imagined showdown between Jack and Billy wouldn't be taking place, but at the same time he was relieved his hide was still standing. He pulled the coat hanger, winching up the door.

"That's the entrance?" Billy chuckled. "It's very small."

"I didn't make it for adults," Twitch said apologetically, dropping to his knees and crawling in. The place looked undisturbed. The hatch up to the viewing platform was closed, and there was no sign of a gang of boys having been inside.

"This is where I watch the birds," Twitch said, propping open the window. "You can see right across the pond."

Billy came and peered out. He had to stoop to avoid bumping his head on the ceiling. "This is next-level stuff," he whistled as he looked about. "You built this by yourself?"

Twitch nodded.

"What's through there?"

"The triangle room has a waterproof roof so I can sleep out here. And that's my fire pit."

Billy didn't reply. He was studying the ferns on the ground in the bedroom. "When did you last sleep here?"

"I haven't yet," Twitch admitted. "I don't think Mum will let me, not whilst there's a murderer on the loose."

"Well, someone has," Billy observed, pointing to the ferns. "Broken stems and crushed leaves."

Twitch came over, his mouth dropping open as he realized Billy was right. "But who would sleep..." He gazed at Billy with wide eyes and whispered, "Do you think it's *Robber Ryan*?"

"Could be."

"Should we tell the police?"

"What will we say? Excuse me, Officer, but Twitch here found some crushed leaves in his den. We think Robber Ryan might be using it to kip in." Billy laughed and shook his head. "They'd think we were half-cut. We need to be certain. It might just be your old friend Jack and his mates larking about."

"But how can we be certain?"

"Set a few traps. Plant a few snares." Billy winked.

Twitch felt a thrill of excitement. Billy *had* to be an undercover policeman. It would be brilliant to go back to school in the autumn having helped catch a dangerous criminal. He'd be able to tell everyone that Robber Ryan had been using his hide as a crash pad. That would wipe the smile off Jack's face.

"Do you think the missing money is near by?"

"I think it might be," Billy said, getting down on his knees, a look of fierce concentration on his face. "Now, to get in here, you have to crawl. So on our way out, we'll take a fern and brush this bit of ground smooth; that way, anyone crawling in will leave a mark."

"We could wind blades of grass across the edge of the door," Twitch suggested. "If someone pulls the coat hanger and lifts the flap, the grass will snap. That way, you'll be able to see from outside that someone's used it and it will warn you that someone could be inside."

"Very good." Billy nodded and Twitch felt a flush of pleasure.

"We need something that can be used as evidence," Billy mused, biting his bottom lip.

"Brambles could work."

"Brambles?"

"The police must already have Ryan's DNA, right? Well, if he's coming at night, he won't be able to see much as he crawls through the door. We could cut three or four long bramble runners and stretch them across the ground, so that his trousers and hands get scratched by the brambles. It'll draw blood and snag his clothes. We can give them to the police and they'll be able to match it to Ryan's DNA."

"Are you some kind of detective?" Billy looked impressed. "That's genius, that is. Go pick some brambles. Real sharp ones."

Twitch went foraging for bramble runners, returning with five good spiky pieces and a few scratches for his efforts. Billy laid them across the doorway, burying each end to hold them close to the ground and dusting a bit of soil on top to hide them. They were careful when leaving the hide, sweeping the ground with a fern branch, closing the door and tying a piece of grass across each side. The door was well and truly booby-trapped.

"I've a good mind to sit and wait," Billy muttered.

"But what if he sees you? You might scare him away," Twitch pointed out.

"You're right. We'll come back tomorrow," Billy grunted.

"Billy, look, it's the baby oystercatcher, and there's the dad." Twitch craned his neck till he spotted the mother, and turned, smiling, but Billy was still staring at the hide. "Look, it's the whole oystercatcher family."

"Yeah, great." Billy nodded but didn't look, and Twitch frowned. He couldn't put his finger on what it was that bothered him about Billy, but for someone who kept professing to like bird-spotting, he hadn't shown any real interest in them. Twitch thought about his words from earlier that afternoon. *Accept that most people will disappoint you,* he'd said. *"I'm a rotten human being."*

He'd seemed to be joking, but what if he hadn't been? Despite the warm afternoon, Twitch felt cold. Why would Billy pretend to like birds if he didn't? What was the point in lying?

By the time they were making their way back across

the boggy ground to the rabbit trail, it was getting on for dinner time.

"Have you gone to look for the kingfishers yet?" Twitch asked.

"Not yet."

"Do you want me to show you where the nests are?"

"Not now."

Twitch huffed, exasperated. "Everyone says they want to see a kingfisher," he muttered, "but no one actually looks for them."

"I do want to see them; it's just that I have things to do."

"Jack said he wanted to see kingfishers, but he never showed up."

"We're back on Jack, are we?" Billy rolled his eyes.

"Ava and Tippi wanted to see the kingfishers – I even marked the nesting sites on their map – but when I offered to take them, they didn't want to go either and—"

Billy stopped walking. "Who are Ava and Tippi? School friends?"

"No, they live on a canal boat called the *Kingfisher*, which is also their surname, and they said they'd come to Aves Wood to see kingfishers, but—"

"A canal boat. That's cool." Billy started walking again. "Where's it moored?"

"Further up the canal, after Aves Lock."

Billy's lips curled, exposing a wide toothy grin, and Twitch suddenly felt uneasy. "Why do you want to know?"

"I don't." Billy shrugged. "I was just letting you get all your kingfisher rage off your chest."

"Oh."

"If you must know, I'm planning to go and look for the kingfishers first thing tomorrow morning."

"You are?"

"Yes. Nice and early, when there's no one about. Best time to catch a kingfisher."

"Yes." Twitch swallowed. His chest felt tight. There was something unnerving about the way Billy was behaving, but he couldn't put his finger on what it was. Twitch reminded himself that he'd spent most of the day with Billy and the man had been kind, and not once been threatening. Setting the traps around the door of the hide had been fun, but the way he was talking right now was odd.

"Let's meet after lunch tomorrow to check our traps," Billy said. "Say two thirty at Bridd Bridge?"

"OK, great." Twitch agreed.

As they came out of the kissing gate onto the towpath, they were about to part ways when Twitch spotted a pair of swifts scything through the air above the water. They dropped, disappearing into a hole in the crumbling canal wall, then burst out like rockets, rising, wheeling and turning at dazzling speed. He remembered Billy saying they were his favourite bird.

"Look, Billy." Twitch pointed. "That family of *sparrows* are having midges for dinner. Do you see? They're nesting in the wall of the canal."

They stood and watched the swifts for a few minutes, Twitch holding his breath, waiting for Billy to correct him.

"Gotta love sparrows," Billy said, nodding. "See you tomorrow, Twitch."

20

AMITA'S ALLOTMENT

Twitch was ready for Amita when the doorbell rang the next morning. The allotments were a twenty-minute walk away and Amita passed the time sharing her family news and gossip. There were staffing issues at her granddaughter's nursery, and her eldest son was suffering from a bad back.

Twitch nodded and made interested noises, but he wasn't really listening. He'd had a night of fitful dreams, and this morning he'd woken up feeling like he had a jigsaw puzzle in his head that wouldn't let him do anything else until he'd fitted all the pieces together. Who was Billy? Was he an undercover policeman? Could Twitch ask him that? Why did he want to know about Tippi and Ava's boat? What were those two girls up to? Why hadn't Jack turned up to spot kingfishers with him when he said he would? Why had Billy told him that he was a birdwatcher, when he didn't know the difference between a swift and a sparrow? Why was everyone lying to him? It seemed to be a puzzle hinging on birds. He wondered, was it anything to do with the *jail*bird who was hiding in Briddvale? Or was that just a coincidence?

"… have you ever felt that way? Hmm?" Amita stopped walking and looked at him for an answer.

"Um … er … yes," Twitch replied, having no idea what the question was.

"Then the best thing to do is fart it out," Amita said, nodding gravely. "Trapped wind can be very painful. Sometimes people think they are dying of appendicitis, but really it's a bubble of air in the wrong place." She patted her tummy. "Ah, look, here we are." She punched her code into the metal number lock on the gate and pushed it open.

Each allotment plot informed on the person who worked it. Some were rectangular, neat and regimented; others had bushy borders or were overgrown. Amita had two plots, as she was tending one for a friend who'd fallen ill. In her own plot she grew fruit and veg, but in the second she'd sown wild flowers and it was humming with insects. An apple tree stood between the plots, a swing hanging from its largest branch.

Taking a key from her pocket, she shuffled to her shed, which she'd painted bright pink much to the consternation of the more conservative allotmenteers, and unlocked the door. Twitch rolled out the wheelbarrow and fetched the fork.

"I will sit here to watch you work and tell you what to do." Amita sat down on the swing. "I'm an old lady, you know. I get tired." She swung back and forth, looking as happy as any four-year-old in a play park.

Twitch grinned. Amita always made a great show of how she was going to boss him around while she rested, but he knew from experience that she'd be on her feet within minutes, tugging up fledgling weeds, checking the progress of growing vegetables and talking to them, as if they were all her children, as she quenched their thirst. She'd ask his advice about what to do with a plant, or a patch of free soil, and then ignore it, doing what she'd always intended to do. And it was in this way that several pleasant sunny hours passed and the wheelbarrow filled up with potatoes, courgettes, tomatoes, onions, bunches of cut herbs, peas, beans and raspberries.

Unable to eat everything she grew, Amita always made Twitch take home a good portion of it. The rest she parcelled up and delivered to neighbours in exchange for a cup of tea and a natter.

"How are your feathered lodgers doing?" Amita asked, referring to Twitch's bedroom swallows.

"Their first chicks have fledged and there are more eggs in the nest."

"It is a miracle that they come to see you year after year."

"I know." Twitch put his foot on the fork and turned up a huddle of new potatoes. Shaking off the earth, he set them gently on the ground to make a pile. The newly disturbed soil writhed as a tangle of worms tried to wriggle away from the sunlight. A robin landed beside them and took a fat one in its beak. It was unusual to see a robin at this time of year. In the summer, they hid whilst they moulted, refreshing their feathers when food was plentiful and the weather warm.

"Is that my robin?" Amita craned her neck. "My little companion? We put the world to rights, he and I. In spring he sang to me, telling me to plant more soft fruit, but he's been a bit quiet of late."

"Robins don't like to sing whilst they're moulting," Twitch told her. "They don't want to attract the attention of a predator when they can't fly away."

"If anything tried to attack my robin..." Amita

shook her fist and Twitch laughed. "A little bird tells me that you've got a new companion, hmm?" She waggled her eyebrows. "Iris says you have a friend called Jack."

"He's just a boy from school."

"It's good you have friends. Companionship lifts the spirits and friendship makes the impossible seem achievable."

"Yeah, well, he's not my friend." Twitch stamped the fork into the ground. "He's my enemy."

"My goodness, how dramatic." She leaned forward, her eyes alight with interest. "What terrible thing did he do?"

"We were meant to look for kingfishers together, but he never showed up."

She tipped back, blowing a raspberry. "This is not a crime worthy of making an enemy."

"Yeah, but then I found him with some other boys, and they were making fun of me."

"You confronted him, yes? What did he say?"

"Pardon?"

"Did he apologize?"

"No."

"And this is why you have made him your enemy." She nodded.

"No, I mean I didn't confront him. He doesn't know I overheard."

"But what if he has a perfectly reasonable explanation?"

"He won't."

"How do you know?"

"It's a dog-eat-dog world. If you're not at the top of the pecking order, you're at the bottom."

"What nonsense is this?" Amita laughed. "When have you ever seen a dog eating another dog? Never, I'll bet."

Twitch was momentarily stunned by this logic.

"You think I don't know what is going on?" She gently cuffed his arm. "I'm a mother of two sons. I know perfectly well what squabbles boys have. People aren't birds, Twitch. They're complicated. They do stupid things. They change their minds. They hurt each other, but it doesn't mean they're not worth understanding." She paused, making sure she had his full attention. "Answer me this question. Would you like Jack to be your friend?"

Twitch wanted to say no, but the truth was he'd enjoyed hanging out with Jack.

"You do, I can see it. Then you must confront him. Give him the opportunity to explain himself.

If it turns out that he was simply having fun at your expense, then we will both count him our enemy and pelt him with rotten tomatoes." She threw a tomato for emphasis and it splattered on the ground, making Twitch smile. "Don't be too hasty to make enemies; it's better not to have any at all." She handed him her secateurs. "Pick those courgettes. They'll be nice and sweet." She sat back down on the swing. "Who told you the world was full of dogs eating other dogs?"

"Billy," Twitch replied, sinking to his knees by the courgette plants.

"I should find this Billy and put him over my knee," she muttered. "He deserves a smacked bottom for such nonsense." She called over to Twitch, "Has it occurred to you that this Billy is jealous of Jack, hmm?"

Twitch laughed. "Billy is a grown-up."

"A grown-up?" Amita looked at Twitch, a serious expression on her face. "From where?"

"Not from around here. He's on holiday, bird-watching." As he said it, Twitch realized he didn't think this was true.

"And what's Billy's surname?"

"I don't know."

"Where's he staying?"

"In a camper van in the bottom field of Patchem's farm."

"Twitch, you are a good and wise boy." Amita stood up. "I'm not going to give you the lecture on strange men who live in vans and don't tell you their surnames, but you should stay away from him. There are bad people in this world, and if you don't know a person's permanent address, or their mother, it is very hard to make them behave themselves."

"I will." Twitch gave her a reassuring smile.

"Mz Ingumook! Mz Ingumook!" came a cry.

Twitch looked up to see a small child running towards them. A few metres behind him was Tara, from school.

"Bazbewees?" The boy grabbed the side of the wheelbarrow and went up on tiptoes to peer in. "Bazbewees?"

"Hello, Darius." Amita bent down to talk to him. "Yes, I have lots of juicy raspberries. Would you like some?"

"Sorry," Tara said, running up. "I took my eyes off him for a second, to help Dad, and he was gone." She kneeled beside her brother and her dark hair tumbled forward. "Darius, you mustn't run off like that." She pushed her hair over her shoulder.

"You mustn't worry, Darius and I are good friends."
Amita chuckled as the boy stuffed a fistful of raspberries
into his mouth, pink juice dripping down his chin.

"Hi." Tara smiled shyly at Twitch.

"Hi," Twitch said, letting his fringe fall over his face
to hide his blushing. "What're you doing here?"

"That's my dad's allotment in the corner." She pointed.

"Twitch has been picking my bountiful harvest."
Amita gestured proudly to the wheelbarrow. "I'm lucky
to have such a strong handsome man to help me, don't
you think?" She squeezed his arm and Twitch's cheeks
burned as Tara giggled.

"More!" Darius held out his chubby hands. "More
bazbewees."

"No, no more," Tara scolded her brother. "C'mon,
let's go back to Daddy and do some digging." She
looked over her shoulder at Twitch and mouthed *thank
you* and *sorry*.

"Quick." Amita had taken an egg box from her shed
and was filling it with raspberries. "Run after her; give
her these for Darius." She leaned close and whispered,
"She's very pretty, hmm?"

Crossing the allotments, Twitch awkwardly thrust
the egg box of raspberries at Tara. "Amita says these are
for Darius."

"Thanks," Tara replied. "I mean, tell Amita thanks."

"OK." Twitch nodded, trying to think of something to say. "I will."

"I saw Jack yesterday, in Aves Wood. He was looking for you. He said you've been hanging out."

Twitch kept nodding, utterly tongue-tied, not knowing how to respond. Jack had been looking for him? An embarrassing silence began to stretch out between them.

"I'm glad you two are friends now."

"He said that?" Twitch's voice was strangled by outrage.

"Yeah. He's nice, isn't he? Once you get to know him." Tara smiled as she nodded, and Twitch felt a slap of jealousy as he realized she liked Jack.

"Only sometimes," he said, and walked away.

21

ROBBER RYAN

When Twitch arrived home, he found a note on the kitchen table from his mum, reminding him that she was going out after work that evening. She wrote that dinner was in the fridge, and that Jack had called by for him, saying he'd try again later. Twitch screwed the paper into a ball and chucked it in the bin. He didn't want to see Jack right now. He was confused. If Jack had been looking for him yesterday, why hadn't he shown up in the morning, like they'd agreed? And he'd promised not to visit the hide unless he was with Twitch, yet he'd gone there and released Squeaker and Frazzle! The laughter of the four boys by the bridge still echoed in his head. No, he wasn't ready to see Jack, and if Jack was going to come back here, he was going out.

Deciding to take the pigeons to the hide for homing practice, Twitch made himself a cheese sandwich to eat there. He emptied all the fruit and veg he'd brought back from the allotment out of Amita's basket and carried it up to the flat roof, grabbing a hand towel on his way through the bathroom. He'd left Jack's trailer in the woods and the cage was up the tree, so the basket would have to do. Amita had been kind about her ruined basket, exacting a dozen eggs as payment, but he would be careful with this one. Remembering the traps he and Billy had set yesterday afternoon, he wondered if the hide had had a night visitor.

Opening the door to the pigeon loft, he picked up Frazzle and put him in the basket, laying the towel over the top as a makeshift lid. The basket wasn't very big. He looked at Squeaker, who was snoozing standing up in her nest box, and wondered whether it would distress her to be crammed in a small basket with her brother. He decided to leave her where she was. Frazzle needed the flying practice more than she did. Twitch pulled a ball of garden twine from his pocket and tied it around the rim of the basket, securing the towel lid.

As he was packing his rucksack, the doorbell rang. Twitch ran along the landing, into his mum's bedroom and peeped round the curtain, looking down at the doorstep.

Jack was standing there, with Ozuru and Terry, carrying a football under his arm. Twitch frowned. Why had Jack brought the other boys to his house? He scanned the street, expecting to see Vernon hiding behind a hedge, waiting to jump him. Jack pointed at Twitch's bike lying in the front garden, and rang the bell again, but when no one answered he shrugged, and the three boys walked away. Jack dropped the ball to the pavement and dribbled it effortlessly up the street.

Of course he's good at football, Twitch thought bitterly, putting on his rucksack and picking up the basket containing Frazzle. He made sure the coast was clear from the top window before going downstairs and climbing on his bike.

He thought about Jack as he cycled to Aves Wood. What did he want? He remembered Amita asking him if he wanted Jack to be his friend, and he knew that he did; but then Billy's voice told him that leopards didn't change their spots, so Amita told Billy that dogs didn't eat dogs, and Billy told her that Twitch should be more goose. They squabbled in his head all the way to the nature reserve, until he was thoroughly confused about what he should do. Watching the birdlife around the pond would help. It was the best place to think. It was where he and Mum had gone, after Grandad had died.

Twitch revelled in the habitual simplicity of being on his own. He left his bike under the bracken blanket and stepped onto his secret path. Moving swiftly and silently, he imagined himself to be changing from a human boy to becoming a part of the wood.

As he approached the hide, his eyes scanned the door for signs of entry, and he halted abruptly. The blades of grass that had been tied across the doorway were snapped. He glanced around nervously, putting Frazzle's basket down. No one was about. He pulled the coat hanger and sank to his knees to examine the ground at the entrance. The previously smoothed earth had been churned by kneecaps and hands. He studied it closely without touching anything and spotted on one of the bramble whips a cotton thread and a drop of congealed blood. He reached into his pocket and pulled out a freezer bag that he'd brought for any evidence. Taking out his penknife, he sliced the piece of bramble that had snagged and cut the knee of whoever had entered the hide, dropping it into the bag and carefully stowing it in his rucksack. His heart beat loudly in his chest, warning him that he might be in danger.

He peered into the den, ready to bolt, but it was empty. Trying not to touch the disturbed earth in the doorway, he clambered in awkwardly, then reached back and grabbed the basket. He wanted to transfer Frazzle into his cage, so he could recover from his journey on the back of the bike before he released him. Twitch suspected that if he let the pigeon go now, he might fly off in any direction.

Shinning up the tree with the basket over his shoulder, Twitch slid onto the platform and carefully put Frazzle into the cage. The pigeon seemed a little confused but perfectly happy and waddled about.

Dropping back down into the hide, Twitch sat on the blue crate to think. His thoughts were whirling and his pulse was galloping. He needed to calm down. Billy had said they should meet back after lunch, because he had something to take care of in the morning. Twitch thought the best thing would be to wait until Billy arrived, show him the triggered traps and ask him straight out if he was an undercover policeman.

He put his hand to his chest, telling his heart there was nothing to be anxious about. He decided to watch the birds around the pond to soothe himself. He pushed the watching window open and yelled, immediately dropping it shut and falling backwards off his crate.

He'd glimpsed a face. Up close. Barely a foot from the window. A shaved head and dark eyes.

Twitch looked about in a panic and grabbed his rucksack, hugging it to his chest. He stared at the door, trembling. There was only one way in and out of the hide. He held his breath, expecting that at any second the door would rise, and Robber Ryan would appear pointing a gun at him. He couldn't breathe, he was so frightened.

"Twitch, come out here," said a soft voice. "I'm not going to hurt you."

Twitch was confused by the voice. Were there two people outside? How did they know his name? Had they been spying on him? Was this some kind of trap?

"I'm stepping back from your den. You can see me from the window," said the voice, and he heard retreating footsteps.

He peeped through the twigs of the window flap, and saw a dark figure moving away. He didn't know what to do. Should he stay inside or go out? He thought about climbing the tree, but then he'd be trapped. At least outside he could run. He quickly pulled his rucksack onto his back, dropped to his knees and, taking a deep breath, crawled out of the door, careful to avoid the bramble snares. He jumped to his feet, his hands curled into fists.

"Hello, Twitch," Robber Ryan said.

Twitch stared at the person in front of him, paralysed by shock. His heart was beating as fast as the wings of a hummingbird and he'd held his breath so long he was becoming dizzy. Everything he'd thought, everything he'd assumed, was thrown into confusion, because the person he was staring at, who was staring back at him, was a *woman*. The highwayman in his imagination disappeared in a puff of smoke. Ryan stood a metre from him, real flesh and murderous blood, with a shaved head, intense eyes, and the long black coat. She was short and athletic, with curves. He gaped at her, hoping he didn't look as terrified as he felt. His knees bent and his feet pushed into the ground as he prepared to run for his life. "How do you know my name?" His voice was a rasp.

"I've come to warn you about that man you were here with yesterday. Please listen to me, Twitch. He's not a good person."

"You've been watching me?" Twitch squeaked.

"Stay away from that man."

"Billy?" Twitch said, taking a step to the side.

"That's not his real name. His real name is Fergal Doherty."

Twitch risked another step. "Why should I believe anything you say?" And another step. "You're Robber Ryan."

"My name's Gwen Ryan, and it's true, I was charged with armed robbery and murder—"

Twitch didn't wait to hear more; he pivoted and ran, as fast and hard as he could, into the woods. He vaulted a fallen tree trunk, hurdled over brambles and dropped suddenly to the forest floor behind a bushy tree, crawling away on his belly to a dip in the ground and pressing his back up against the entrance to a badger sett, gasping for breath.

What was happening? Robber Ryan had been watching him and knew Billy. Billy wasn't Billy; he was Fergal. And Robber Ryan was a woman! Twitch's brain lurched from one puzzle to the next as he tried to get his breath back. He didn't know what was going on any more, but he did know he needed to find a police officer. He peeped over the top of the dip. There was no one coming. Robber Ryan hadn't chased after him.

He got up, keeping low, and made his way as quickly and quietly as he could back to the main footpath.

"Twitch? Hey, I was just coming to meet you on the bridge."

Twitch's breath stuck and his heartbeat accelerated as Billy strolled towards him. "Hi," he said brightly, hoping he sounded normal.

"What're you doing?"

Twitch pointed up into the canopy. "Great spotted woodpecker. I was watching it," he lied.

"Where?" Billy came to stand beside him and looked up. "I can't see it."

"You can hear it." Twitch laughed nervously. "There. Did you hear that?"

"Nope." Billy chuckled. "Your ability to spot birds is next level."

"But you love to spot birds too, don't you?" Twitch asked, hoping Billy would suddenly prove his suspicions and the accusations from Gwen Ryan wrong. He realized with an increasing sense of panic that he didn't know who to trust any more. He was terrified, and wanted to be left alone with his birds.

"I spent this morning searching for kingfishers and caught three of them having breakfast." A shark-like smile split Billy's face.

"Really?" A chill lifted the goosebumps on Twitch's arms as he realized Billy wasn't talking about birds.

"It was very … satisfying." He clapped his hands together. "So, shall we go to your hide and see if any of our snares have been triggered?"

"Oh, I've already been," Twitch said in as matter-of-fact a way as he could manage. The chill in Billy's voice focused his mind. "Someone's definitely used it to sleep in. It freaked me out. I didn't want to hang around." He pulled the freezer bag from his rucksack. "I copied what they do on the telly and put the evidence in a bag." He handed it to Billy, who took it and examined the threads and the blood.

"Bingo." His shark-like smile returned.

"Shall we go to the police?" Twitch glanced up the path, praying for an officer to come walking down it.

"Not yet. I'd like to check the hide myself first," Billy threw out his hand. "Lead the way."

"Actually, I bumped into Jack this morning," Twitch lied. "He apologized about yesterday and has invited me to play football with him and his mates. That was what I was coming to tell you. I kind of had to say yes," Twitch gabbled, stepping backwards. "Sorry."

Billy narrowed his eyes. "Right."

"Do you think you can find the hide on your own?"

"I'm sure I can, but, Twitch…"

"Great, just look for the rusty shopping trolley. See

you later," Twitch said cheerfully, turning and walking away fast but not too fast.

"Leave this with me," Billy called out, holding up the freezer bag. "You don't need to do anything; I'll deal with it. I'll talk to the police."

"Got it," Twitch replied, with a thumbs up. "Thanks."

22

BARGE IN

As Twitch walked away from Billy, he told his heart to quieten down. It was louder than his brain, and he needed to think. Yesterday Billy had said that he'd come to Briddvale to hunt for kingfishers, and now he said he'd caught three having breakfast. If he wasn't talking about the birds, there was only one thing he could have meant.

As soon as he was around the corner and out of sight, Twitch broke into a sprint.

Exiting Aves Wood through the kissing gate, he powered up the towpath, the muscles in his legs burning from the exertion. He felt a powerful shock of relief when he saw the *Kingfisher* moored up where it had been on Sunday. But as he got closer to the boat his senses prickled. It was the middle of the afternoon: why were all the curtains closed? Perhaps Ava, Tippi and Nan had gone out on a sketching expedition, or a picnic. He leaned over the side of the boat and banged on the cabin door.

It swung open.

Looking down, Twitch saw that the lock had been broken. His heart lurched as he peered inside the dark cabin. "Hello?" he called. "Nan? Ava? Tippi? Hello?"

There was no reply.

Stepping onto the boat, he cautiously descended into the main cabin. Empty jam jars were rolling about on the floor, and pens, pencils and paintbrushes were in a pick-up-sticks mess beside them. Gilbert's portrait had tumbled off the easel. Twitch lifted it up and put it back. What had happened in here? It looked like a struggle. Where were the girls?

"Nan? Ava?" he repeated as he opened the corkboard door at the far end of the cabin and looked down the dark corridor, terrified of what he might see. It was empty. He took a step forward, almost screaming when he heard a knocking sound. Rigid as a board and barely breathing, he listened. The knocking sound came again. Tiptoeing forward, he pushed the nearest door open. The bathroom was empty. He crept further along. More knocking.

"Ava? Tippi?" he squeaked, trying to be brave.

He came to the door of another cabin, took a deep breath and pushed it open. He gasped at what he saw inside. On the double bed that took up most of the room were Nan, Tippi and Ava, gagged, blindfolded and tied up, top to tail, with their hands and feet lashed to the bed frame.

The knocking sound was coming from Nan's foot kicking at the bedpost.

"Oh no!" Twitch exclaimed as he rushed forward. He tugged the scarf from Tippi's eyes. "Tippi, it's me. It's Twitch. It's OK," he soothed as he pulled at the tape over her mouth. "I'm sorry," he said, worried that it might hurt, but Tippi had been crying and her salty tears had made the tape gum weak.

"Help," she sobbed.

And Twitch nodded, pulling his penknife from his pocket and sawing at the blue nylon rope that held her hands above her head. When it snapped she sat up and hugged him tight.

"It's OK, Tippi. I'm here now. But you've got to let go. I need to help Nan and your big sister."

Tippi removed Ava's blindfold while he worked at the bindings that held her wrists. Once she was free, she ripped the tape off her face.

"Thank goodness you came!" She sat up, untying

her feet whilst Twitch sawed at Nan's bonds.

"What happened?" he asked Ava, but she didn't reply. She looked at Nan.

"Was it Billy? Did he do this?" Twitch asked Nan, dreading her answer. It had been him who'd told Billy where the boat was.

"Who is Billy?" Tippi asked.

"Listen to me," Nan said, rubbing her wrists. Twitch could see she'd been tied up very tightly; her wrists looked like Jack's had when Twitch had freed him. "We're in danger. There'll be time for explanations when we are safe."

"You think he'll come back?" Ava asked.

Nan nodded. "Almost certainly."

"But why?" Tippi asked, her lips trembling.

"Because we have something that he wants, sweet pea," she said softly, stroking Tippi's cheek.

"What do we do?" Ava asked, alert and ready.

"We need to move the boat." Nan looked at Twitch. "I don't want to drag you into our problems, Twitch. You should go. Thank you for all you have done for us."

"But I want to help," Twitch protested. "What can I do? Shall I get the police?"

"No!" Ava stood up, as if to block his exit.

"We cannot go to the police, Twitch." Nan fixed him with her kind, wise eyes. "If you really want to help us, I need you to trust me. I promise I'll explain everything when we're safe, but we can't go to the police."

"OK." Twitch nodded.

"Now is not the time for talking. Now is a time for action. We need to move this boat as quickly as possible."

"I can help with that."

"Canal boats don't move fast. We'll only get a few hundred metres along the canal before we meet a lock. The *Kingfisher* is pointing downstream. When he finds the boat gone, Fergal will assume we've continued in that direction, because it's easier and faster."

Fergal! Twitch flinched at the name, feeling a stab of guilt. That was what Gwen Ryan had called Billy. It *was* Billy who'd done this. He looked at Ava and Tippi, but said nothing.

"However, we're not going downstream," Nan continued. "We're going to turn this boat around, and head up the canal." She looked at Twitch. "Ava will need help with the lock gates. It takes two, and you're bigger and stronger than Tippi; you'll do it faster."

Twitch nodded, springing to his feet.

"Thank you." She smiled and turned to Ava. "You

two run ahead of the boat and open the gates. I'll swing her round and sail through as fast as possible."

"Let's do it," Ava agreed.

As they hurried back through the main cabin, Twitch noticed that Ava was limping. "Are you all right?" he asked as she handed him a heavy iron L-shaped bar with a square hole at one end.

"I will be when we're safe. That's the key for the lock. We each take a side of the canal. You use the key to let the water in or out of the lock. When the water is level, we open the gates."

"Got it." Twitch nodded, gripping the key tightly, determined not to let her down.

"Let's go." Ava stepped off the boat, wincing when she put weight on her right foot, but she didn't complain.

As they hurried along the towpath, Nan started the *Kingfisher*'s engine and Twitch glanced over his shoulder. Nan was stood at the rear of the boat with her hand on the tiller. Tippi was at the front, reeling out the mooring rope, which was looped through an iron ring cemented into the towpath. He paused to watch as Nan used a pole to push out the back of the boat into the middle of the canal. She revved the engine, then shut it off as the stern swung around, the momentum turning it.

Tippi was waiting on her signal. As the rear of the boat came in line with the opposite bank, there was a crunching sound, and Nan used the pole to push the *Kingfisher* away from the shallow edge and continue its turn. She nodded at Tippi, who released the rope, winding it swiftly back in around her arm, like someone who'd lived on boats all her life. Nimble as a cat, she stepped onto a ridge along the outside of the cabin and ran back to stand beside Nan. The boat was now facing upstream. They'd turned it in under a minute. Twitch had never seen it done so fast.

"Come on!" Ava called to him; she was already a hundred metres down the towpath.

He sprinted to catch up. Twitch saw the kissing gate ahead of them and felt a flutter of panic at the thought that Billy might come through it at any moment. How long had it been since he'd left him on his way to the hide? He had no sense of time.

As soon as they reached Aves Lock, Ava raced across the gate to the other side of the canal. Keeping his eyes on Ava, Twitch copied her, doing exactly what she did, as she slotted the square hole of her lock key over a giant square peg. They both turned their keys, lifting an iron shaft out of the ground and opening a panel in the gates, letting the water roar out of the lock. As soon as the water was level with the canal beyond, they wedged their feet against the concrete ledges in the ground, put their backs against the lock gates and pushed them open. Nan steered the boat into the lock. They closed the gates behind it, then ran to the gates at the front. Again the keys went over the pegs. Again they turned, this time releasing water into the lock, bringing the level up to meet the canal beyond the gates. The *Kingfisher* slowly rose up with the water, except it wasn't the *Kingfisher* any more. Tippi was leaning over the bow of the boat, clipping a blue tarpaulin banner over some unseen hooks. Now the boat's name was the *Suffolk*.

Twitch looked at Nan, her jaw set, her eyes determined, wondering who she really was. What kind of people lived on a boat and carried banners to change its name? And then he realized he knew the answer: people on the run.

23

FLIGHT OF THE *KINGFISHER*

As the boat came out of the lock, Ava and Twitch jumped aboard. They chugged up the canal through Siskin Lock, which was open, and under Crowther Bridge. Twitch kept his eyes fixed on the towpath behind them, watching for Billy. The further they went, the better he felt, but the boat seemed to be going so slowly and he wouldn't be able to relax until there was a good distance between them and the man with two names. As they passed the pipe works, Ava signalled that there was another lock coming up. Nan steered the boat close to the bank. Twitch and Ava jumped off, running ahead with their keys.

In this manner, the *Kingfisher* passed through Plover Lock, Dotterel Lock and Linnet Lock until they reached a huge lock that looked like a guillotine and had to be operated by a machine with a push button. Nan steered the boat into the basin beyond, so it was sandwiched between the first two of the three locks at Petrel.

"We'll moor up here." Nan gestured towards the opposite bank and a space in the middle of a row of boats.

"How far have we come?" Tippi asked.

"Nearly three miles," Twitch replied.

Nan nodded across the water. "There's a pub over there. We'll be safest amongst people."

Ava and Tippi hopped off the boat, one at the bow, one at the stern, each holding a rope. They threaded them through the mooring rings and tied them tight. Nan shut down the engine, closed up and locked the hatch door at the back of the boat before following Twitch and the girls down into the main cabin.

Tippi had been tidying whilst Nan had been steering; all the stuff that was on the floor was back in the right place.

"Hot milk with sugar for everyone," Nan announced, putting a pan on the stove and emptying two pints of milk into it.

Twitch nodded. He suddenly felt tired, rinsed out by the adrenaline that had been coursing round his body. The morning at the allotment with Amita felt like months ago.

Nan dropped a teaspoon of sugar into four mugs, then poured in the hot milk, giving them all a stir before bringing them over to the table where the children were sat.

"Are we OK?" She looked at each of them in turn.

Tippi nodded. "Better now, Nan."

"That's a good brave girl. Ava?"

"I've hurt my ankle," she replied with a weak smile. "I jarred it, kicking him."

"We'll strap it up," Nan promised, and then she turned to Twitch. "Are you OK, Twitch?" she asked kindly.

And suddenly Twitch realized that he wasn't. He struggled to reply, not wanting to cry. "This is all my fault," he whispered.

"Now, now, it's nobody's fault."

"Yes, it is," Ava interrupted. "It's Fergal Doherty's fault."

Nan closed her eyes and sighed. "Well, yes. It is his fault" – she looked at Twitch – "but it's not yours. Why would you think it was?"

"I told Billy, I mean Fergal, where your boat was. I didn't know he'd do this ... I didn't know..."

"Calm yourself. Let's start at the beginning. Are you saying that you know Fergal, and he's been calling himself Billy?"

Twitch took a deep breath and told them how he'd met a man called Billy four days ago, who'd come to his rescue when he was being bullied and claimed to be interested in birdwatching, and who he'd thought might be an undercover policeman.

"Jack tried to make you eat a worm!" Ava scowled. "What a bully!"

He described the conversation where Billy and he were talking about kingfishers that had led to him mentioning the girls and betraying the location of their boat.

"But how did you find out that Billy and Fergal were the same person?" Ava asked.

Twitch paused, looking at each of their faces in turn. "I met a woman outside my hide, in Aves Wood. She had a shaved head. She told me Billy's real name was Fergal, that he was bad news and I should stay away from him."

"Mummy!" Tippi clapped.

"Your *mother* is Robber Ryan?" Twitch exclaimed.

"Please don't call her that," Ava snapped. "She's not a robber; she's innocent."

"I'm sorry. I..." Twitch shook his head, not knowing what to say. He wondered if he should feel frightened, but he was tired of being scared, and the warm milk was comforting. He didn't feel threatened by Nan or Ava, and Tippi was sweet.

"Mum met Fergal Doherty four years after Dad died," Ava said. "He was funny and nice to us. Although Nan never liked him."

"Nan is Dad's mum," Tippi explained.

"Mum dated Fergal for nearly six months, then, the next thing we knew, Mum was arrested for armed robbery and suspected murder." She looked at Twitch. "And it's all Fergal's fault."

"Mummy never did any robbing," Tippi protested, shaking her head.

"Fergal is the head of a gang of thieves," Ava said. "He masterminded the robbery of that armed security van. The driver was in on it. They'd been planning it for months. The day of the robbery, Fergal asked to borrow Mum's car. He told her he had a job interview." She paused to control her anger. "Mum is an osteopath. She has a room at this alternative therapies place. That day, she had a full diary of bookings, but none of her clients showed up. She sat in her room waiting for her appointments to arrive, but they didn't because he had cancelled them all." She looked at Twitch. "Do you know what that meant?"

Twitch shook his head.

"It meant she had no alibi for the time of the robbery. Fergal planned it that way. He did the robbery with his gang in a truck. They dumped it and loaded all of the stolen money into Mum's car. They split up to avoid capture. He was meant to meet them later, but Fergal had a different plan. He drove back to our house, which was empty because we were at school and Mum was at work." She breathed in through her nose and out through her mouth.

"Fergal smashed up our house. He made it look like there'd been a big fight, even leaving drops of his own blood and pulling out his hair." She scowled. "Once he was done, he drove to Kittiwake Cliff. He parked Mum's car, took off his shoes and coat and threw them over the edge. He roughed up the inside of the car, making sure his handprints and blood would be easy to find, then changed into a disguise, a smart suit and dark wig. He dropped Mum's car back home, walked round the corner to where he had a rental car waiting, and made his escape."

"The person your mum is accused of murdering is Fergal Doherty?" Twitch was shocked.

Ava nodded. "His body was never found, because he isn't dead, but all the circumstantial evidence of the fight – Fergal's blood and his hair, his shoes washing up down the coast – it was enough for a jury to convict her. They said she fought with him about the money and threw him off the cliff to his death."

"That's awful! But wait, I don't understand. What about the money? The papers said that your mum had hidden it. If Fergal escaped with it, why is he here now living in a camper van?"

"That's the only bit the papers did get right." Ava looked at Nan.

"I think we can trust Twitch," Nan said with a nod.

"Mum couldn't understand why her clients weren't showing up to their appointments," Ava said. "Normally she kept her work stuff in her car, but she'd lent it to Fergal. That morning, she'd taken her work bag out of the boot and left it in our hall. Her appointments book was in there. After three no-shows, she cycled home to fetch it and called a few of her clients. All of their appointments had been cancelled by a male assistant she didn't have. She couldn't understand what was going on.

"School called her. I wasn't feeling very well, and since she no longer had any appointments, she said she'd come and collect me. She left the house and was at the end of the road when she saw Fergal drive up and park. She figured she could use her car to come and get me, so she walked back. But when she arrived, he was smashing up the house. Cleverest thing she did was not go inside. She had her spare set of car keys in her handbag. She opened the driver's door, saw a gun on the passenger seat and got scared. She checked the boot and found five black duffel bags full of money. She grabbed them and threw them into the neighbour's front garden, shut the boot and hid with them behind the hedgerow. Fergal came out, got in the car and drove off to the cliffs."

"Without the money?"

"Exactly." Ava nodded.

"What did your mum do next?"

"She called a cab, put the money in it, then picked up both me and Tippi from school. She realized Fergal was framing her for something, because of all the fake appointments, so she took us and the bags to a hotel. Then she left to find out what was going on. That's how we know about Fergal's disguise and his returning the car."

"But Mummy never came back," Tippi said sadly.

"Nan arrived a few hours later," Ava continued. "Mum had called her from the police station. She had been arrested, charged with masterminding the robbery and killing Fergal."

"So Fergal has come to Aves Wood looking for your mum so he can get his stolen money back?" They all nodded. "And your mum's been sleeping in my hide for the past couple of nights?"

"We followed you, and found it for her," Tippi said proudly.

"It's a really good camp," Ava added.

"But why haven't the police caught her yet?"

"That first day, when they were searching Aves Wood, Gwen was hiding on our boat," Nan said, "and we kept moving."

"But why go to the garage? It was that picture in the newspapers that gave away her hiding place."

"She went to that garage on purpose. She knew she would be caught on CCTV, that the news websites and papers would publish the photo, and that would bring Fergal to Briddvale."

"But why would you want him here?"

"To trap him," Ava said. "Mum grew up in Briddvale. She knows Aves Wood like the back of her hand. She chose it because she thought she could evade capture long enough to draw Fergal into the woods. If we can prove Fergal Doherty is alive and that he stole the money, Mum will be acquitted and can come home. Life can go back to normal."

"We won't have to hide any more," Tippi said.

"Each morning we go into the woods and take her a new disguise," Ava said.

Twitch remembered them hiding the first time he'd seen them, when Ava had dropped her bracelet, and then seeing them with a blonde woman. His mind was fizzing as things that hadn't made sense all suddenly connected.

"We take Mummy food, and we have picnics, like normal families do," Tippi said.

"The police aren't looking for a normal family," Ava added.

"So Billy, I mean Fergal..." A horrible thought occurred to him. "Oh no, Ava, he knows about my hide. I showed it to him." He looked at Nan. "He knows Gwen's been sleeping there. I think he came to the boat and tied you up because he's planning to use you to blackmail her into giving him the money! He's there *right now*!"

24

GIVING A HOOT

"It won't work," Ava said calmly. "Mum doesn't have the money." She turned to Nan. "What should we do now?"

Nan looked at him. "Twitch, I need your help one last time." He nodded. "How far away do you live?"

"About a mile from here."

"Does Fergal know where you live?"

"I don't think so."

"Good. Take Tippi and Ava to your house and keep them safe whilst I deal with him." She turned to Ava. "I'll come and get you when it's over."

"What!" Ava was on her feet. "No!"

"Please, Ava," Nan said sternly. "I cannot leave you on the boat; it's not safe. He knows what it looks like, and there's no lock on the door now."

"Let Twitch take Tippi. I want to help."

Nan shook her head. "I want you both to go with Twitch. If Fergal gets his hands on you, he'll be able to make me and your mother do whatever he wants. You need to be somewhere safe. First, I need to secure the boat, find a locksmith or at least borrow a good padlock, then I'm going to help your mother catch that crafty fox and prove she's innocent."

Ava glared at Nan, saying nothing. Then she nodded reluctantly.

"Why is locking the boat so important?" asked Twitch.

"I think it's time we took Twitch into our confidence. He should know everything. Show him, Ava."

Ava motioned for Twitch to follow her. She took him down the hallway to the back of the boat and pointed to a small narrow door to the right of the steps up to the back deck where Nan stood to steer the boat. "Open it." She handed him a key that she'd taken from a pot shaped like an owl.

"What's in there?" Twitch asked, turning the key in the lock.

"The engine room."

The stench of diesel curled Twitch's nostrils as he opened the door. Piled on the floor in front of the grease-smeared engine were five duffel bags.

"Open the top one. Look inside."

Twitch pulled back the zip and gasped at the sight of stacks and stacks of fifty-pound notes, gathered in bundles. "Is this...?"

Ava nodded. "It's the money Fergal stole." She stepped back. "Close the bag and lock the door."

Twitch's mind was reeling. Question after question begged to be asked, but he could see from the look on Ava's face that this was a test.

"Now do you see why Nan needs to lock the boat?"

Twitch nodded. "Is that five million pounds?"

"Every penny that was stolen is there," she said defensively. "We haven't spent any of it. We need it to clear Mum's name."

The three children left the boat with Twitch leading the way back along the canal. When they reached Linnet Lock, he explained that they could cross and take a short cut through the fields to Briddvale Road and be at his house in twenty minutes.

Ava shook her head. "We're not going back to your house." She looked defiant. "We're going to find Mum."

Tippi moved to stand beside her big sister, nodding. "Fergal will tell Mum he tied me and Ava up. She'll be worried about us."

"Come on, we don't have time to hang around." Ava took her sister's hand and they continued down the towpath, towards Aves Wood. Twitch followed after them, not sure what to do.

Late afternoon was sliding into early evening. Tippi's legs got tired from the fast pace. They stopped for a rest on a crumbling dry stone wall. Twitch gazed up at the sky, putting his hands in his pockets. They'd be losing the daylight in a couple of hours. His fingers touched a scrunched-up bit of paper. Taking it out, he saw it was the message Jack had attached to Squeaker's leg. He felt a flush of guilt at not having read it yesterday and unfurled it.

T – Billy said I missed you this morning. I thought you'd go to the hide. I saw Frazzle and Squeaker in their cage and assumed you were inside. But you aren't. Guessing you're at home, so sending you this message. Hope that's OK? Pigeon post is AWESOME! Sorry we didn't get to spot kingfishers. How about tomorrow? – J

Twitch frowned. *Billy had spoken to Jack?* When Twitch had bumped into him on the path that morning, he'd said that he hadn't seen Jack. A surge of anger pushed him to his feet. Billy had lied. That meant Jack *had* been coming to meet him. He was mucking about under the bridge with the others because he thought Twitch had gone! But why would Billy lie to him?

Thinking back to when he'd first met the man, Twitch realized he'd been unconsciously helping Billy ever since he'd arrived in Briddvale. *"You might know a lot about birds, kiddo, but you don't seem to know a lot about people."* Billy had been manipulating him! He'd used him to find out where to hide his van. He'd used him to find out what was going on in Aves Wood. He'd used him to find out about the Kingfishers; and he'd used him to get to Gwen Ryan. Twitch had been very helpful to Billy indeed.

Clamping his teeth together, Twitch drew in a deep breath. He'd put Ava, Tippi and Nan in danger. He might have lost Jack as a friend. And, right now, Gwen Ryan was facing Billy alone in Aves Wood. He needed to make this right. He was going to help clear Gwen Ryan's name and put Fergal Doherty behind bars where he belonged, and then he'd apologize to Jack.

"C'mon," he said to Ava, "we don't have much light left. We need to get a move on if we're going to help your mum."

Ava looked surprised, and glanced at Tippi, who grinned, and they stood up.

"Follow me. I know the quickest way."

The three of them hurried through the car park into the woods, ignoring the paths. Twitch stopped them amongst the trees before the pond; above it, the sky was blushing red. "When we move across this bit of ground, we'll be visible to anyone who comes out of the hide or looks out the window. We have to keep low and stick to the water's edge so that the reeds hide us, but that means the risk of sinking into the pond is high. You need to follow me footstep for footstep." He glanced anxiously at Tippi but she looked as determined as her big sister.

"Come on," Ava said impatiently, and he could see she was worrying about her mother.

"Wait." Twitch unzipped his rucksack and took out his binoculars. He pointed them across the pond at the hide and turned the dial so that the image came into focus. He watched for a moment and then passed them to Ava. "They're both inside. The door's open, and I can see feet. One person is standing – I think Billy – and another is sitting."

Ava snatched the glasses, looking for the longest time. Then she smiled. "I saw Mum's feet move," she said to Tippi. "She's OK."

Twitch led them carefully and quietly across the

marshy reed bog. As they crept closer to the hide, he realized he had no idea what they were going to do when they got there. He thought of Billy shadow-boxing and lifting weights and knew they wouldn't be able to fight him. Billy could knock them all over with one sweep of his muscly arms. He glanced nervously at Tippi; she was so little. He wished he'd taken her home, like Nan had said, but it was too late now.

"Listen," he whispered. "My house is number fifty-five – the number of fingers you have on each hand – and I live on Sunningdale Street. You got that? Sunningdale Street." Tippi and Ava nodded. "In my front garden there's a plant pot with a climbing rose that grows around the door. In it is a statue of a flamingo. Under it is a key to my house. If anything happens to any of us, you go to my house and let yourself in. OK? My mum's out tonight, so there'll be no one there."

Ava and Tippi both nodded. He could see they were as nervous as he was. The closer they got to the hide, the harder the pulse throbbed in his neck. No matter how much time Twitch spent outdoors, he was always astonished at how quickly dusk passed into night. The mosquitoes and midges were buzzing about his ears, delighted that such fleshy prey was at the water's edge where they laid their eggs. He wished he had his insect repellent on and slapped his hand against his neck, squashing a sucker dead.

They were barely ten metres from the hide when a barn owl, out hunting for mice, emitted a blood-curdling squeal and Tippi jumped, losing her footing. As the ground gave way, she screamed and screamed, sinking up to her waist in cold water.

"Tippi!" Ava gasped, grabbing her sobbing sister and hauling her out.

Twitch had gone rigid with fear. Sound carried across water and Tippi's screams had been loud. Billy's face appeared in the doorway of the hide. He'd heard her.

"This isn't going to work," Twitch hissed at Ava, trying to keep the panic from his eyes. "We should call the police. They'll see Fergal is alive and let your mum go."

Ava shook her head vehemently. "No, they'll think Mum and Fergal were working together. We need him to confess in front of a witness."

"OK." Twitch swallowed. "I'll go to the hide and tell your mum you're OK. Get Tippi somewhere safe. Like Nan said, if he catches you, then he can make your mum do whatever he wants, right?"

Ava nodded. Her eyes were wide. She was looking

over his shoulder. "He's coming," she whispered, hugging Tippi to her.

"Right." Twitch stepped into the pond up to his middle. "You stay here and don't make a sound. Once I'm in the hide, you take Tippi to my house and wait there for me, OK?"

"But—"

"Just do it," Twitch hissed, and he waded towards Billy without looking back.

"Billy," he called out, once he was a good distance from the girls. "Help me!"

Billy looked about, but then spotted Twitch waist-deep in pond water. A feline grin spread across his face and Twitch could see he was relieved. "What happened to you?"

"Jack tricked me." He looked down, hoping he seemed sad. "There wasn't any football game. I went to the playing field, but no one was there."

"I told you; you don't need friends like that."

"I know." He sighed. "I thought I'd come back and watch the birds for a bit, but as I was coming over a barn owl cried out right behind me and startled me. I tripped and..." He splashed his hands down on the water in frustration. "Now I'm soaked. What are you still doing here?"

"Give me your hand." Billy reached out and grabbed Twitch's wrist, pulling him out of the pond, but he didn't let go; instead he twisted round swiftly, yanking Twitch's wrist up behind his back.

"Ow!" Twitch cried out. "What are you doing?"

"Shut it," Billy hissed. "Make another sound and you'll regret it."

25

MESSAGE IN A CAPSULE

Billy shoved Twitch into the hide, letting go of his wrist. Twitch fell on his face. When he sat up, he saw Gwen Ryan on the ground in the triangle room. Her hands were tied, and there was a lantern beside her. He locked eyes with her, hoping to communicate an unspoken alliance, make it clear that Billy was an enemy to both of them, but her expression was blank.

"Now, where was I?" Billy snarled.

"Who's that?" Twitch asked.

"That," Billy replied with a smirk, "is *Robber* Ryan."

"But she's a woman!"

"Yes."

"But we talked about Robber Ryan lots. You never once said she was a woman. I thought Robber Ryan was a man."

"I know you did, but you were wrong."

"But—"

"Shut up!" Billy snapped, turning back to Gwen, whose face was still blank. "This boy, he's the one who led me to your daughters. And now they're blindfolded, gagged and bound tightly." He leaned down and whispered menacingly, "They're really scared right now, and they should be, because if you don't tell me where that money is, they're going to get hurt."

A shadow darkened Gwen Ryan's face, but her expression didn't change, and she said nothing.

"It if wasn't for Twitch, I might never have found them."

"Found who?" Twitch asked, playing dumb.

"The Kingfisher girls," Billy replied.

"What?" Twitch acted shocked. "Where have you taken them?"

"I didn't have to take them anywhere." He swung back to Gwen. "They're trussed up like chickens on that boat of theirs."

"But you moved the boat?" Twitch insisted.

"No." Billy was becoming irritated by Twitch's interruptions. "I didn't need to. They're tied up in the cabin."

"But the boat's gone," Twitch said, looking at Gwen, hoping she understood that he was trying to tell her the girls were safe.

"What?" Billy swung round and Twitch flinched, allowing his fear to show on his face.

"On my way back from the playing field, I passed the place where their boat had been moored this morning. It's gone."

Billy stared at him, and Gwen laughed, low and quiet.

"Why, you little…" Billy grabbed Twitch by his shirt and lifted him off the floor.

"I didn't do anything," Twitch cried out.

"Fergal," Gwen said, "put the boy down."

Billy threw Twitch to the ground, knocking the air out of his lungs.

"Fergal?" Twitch gasped. "Who's Fergal?"

"Me," Billy said with a mean smile.

"But your name's Billy!" Twitch protested, wrapping his arms protectively across his chest.

"Actually, it's Fergal William Doherty, but plenty of people called me Billy when I was a kid. You can call me what you like."

"You didn't come to Briddvale to watch birds, did you?" Twitch said accusingly. "You were after Robber Ryan's money all along."

"That's *my* money!" Billy shouted, advancing towards Twitch, who scuttled backwards until he could feel a tepee tent pole against his back.

"Aren't you curious about how your money disappeared?" Gwen asked, stopping Billy in his tracks.

His head snapped round and he kicked the blue crate closer to the opening of the triangular room, sitting on it with his back to Twitch, blocking the hide's exit. "I'm all ears, sweetheart."

Gwen gave him a sour look. "Don't call me sweetheart."

Billy laughed.

Slowly and silently, Twitch rose to his feet. Gwen glanced at him and he put his finger to his lips. He couldn't get out of the hide through the door. Billy was sat right in front of it, so the only way to go was up.

"You thought your plan was foolproof, didn't you?" Gwen said, locking eyes with Billy so he didn't turn round. "Must have been galling to have faked your own death and then discover you didn't have a penny to your new fake name." She smiled coldly.

"Not as galling as being put in prison for crimes you didn't commit," Billy retorted. He shrugged. "I'll admit. It wasn't what I'd planned."

Twitch took a tiny step towards the tree trunk, and then another, moving slowly, as if he were approaching a nervous bird.

"I knew you were up to something," Gwen said.

"You're a good liar, I'll give you that, but I'd already decided to end our relationship."

"As had I." Billy gave a wolfish laugh.

"Were you always planning to rob your fellow thieves, as well as the security van?"

"You must know there's no honour amongst thieves, Gwen."

"But when did you decide to pin it all on me?"

"The night I met you in that bar, I was looking for the person I was going to frame for my murder. I wanted someone tough enough that you'd believe they were capable of murder, someone clever enough to have plotted a robbery, but dumb enough not to see what I was up to. You fitted the bill perfectly."

Twitch had reached the trunk. He pressed his back against it as he stretched up and carefully opened the hatch in the roof.

"Well, you got the first two right." Gwen gave him a bitter smile. "Juries don't like a woman with a shaved head, and I never thought you'd be capable of armed robbery. You lay on the Irish charm so thick."

"To be sure, to be sure," Billy replied, mocking her.

Twitch lifted his right foot onto the low stubby branch and, transferring his weight forward, he reached up and caught hold of the branch above.

"I was confused, sat there in my treatment room, wondering why none of my clients were showing up for their appointments. I wanted to call them and check, but I'd left my diary at home. So, I went back to get it."

"I thought you must have." Billy nodded.

Twitch lifted his left foot off the ground, holding his breath, expecting any second to hear Billy shout at him. He moved his body up the trunk as slowly as a sloth, trying to stay calm. It took all the strength he had in his arms to haul his legs up and out of the hatch silently.

"I saw you arrive at the house. I was down the end of the road. By the time I reached the front door, you were smashing up the place. I was going to drive off in the car – I had the spare set of keys, you see – but then I saw the gun on the passenger seat and got frightened. I checked the boot, not knowing if I'd find a dead body. You can imagine my surprise to see five big bags stuffed with money. I threw them into the Joneses' front garden, next door." Twitch saw her smile. "I hid there too, and watched you as you strutted to the car, grinning from ear to ear. I was terrified you'd check the boot. But you didn't. I watched you drive away. Then I called a cab."

Twitch reached down and lowered the roof hatch behind him, closing it softly. He couldn't afford one slip. Careful not to make a sound, he climbed up the tree to the pigeon platform, and to Frazzle.

Twitch couldn't make out Billy's words but he heard the anger in his voice. Then he heard him shout, "You're going to tell me where that money is, or I'll hurt the boy."

Gwen laughed, then said, nice and loud so Twitch could hear, "He squeezed out of the door behind you ten minutes ago. He's long gone."

"What!" Billy yelled, and then Twitch heard him swear.

Twitch dug out his penknife and cut through two young green branches thick with leaves. He sat back beside the cage, propping the branches in front of him so he was hidden. Frazzle strutted towards him and cooed, pecking at his sleeve. Slipping his hand into the pocket of his army combats, Twitch pulled out some seed and poured a little mound in front of the bird. The pigeon ate it hungrily.

Billy exploded out of the hide below, looking left then right. He scratched his head, puzzled by Twitch's vanishing act. After searching around for a while in vain, he lost his temper and took it out on a nearby tree, kicking and punching it, swearing angrily. When he was done, his knuckles were dark with blood.

Paralysed with fear, Twitch watched Billy return. The man glanced up at the tree, but he didn't see Twitch hidden amongst its branches. Twitch silently thanked the stars that he was wearing camo.

The horizon was stained plum purple as the last of the sun's beams were soaked up by the rotating Earth, and it was getting darker by the minute. Twitch shivered. His trousers were still wet from standing in the pond. He realized that unless Billy left, or someone came to rescue him, he was going to be stuck up the tree all night. No one knew where he was except Ava and Tippi. The only other person aware of the location of his hide was Jack – whom he'd pushed away so far he'd probably never come back. He looked about to see if he could climb across to another tree, but there were no branches close enough that would hold his weight and it was too dark to risk a jump.

"Oh, Frazzle," he murmured, "we're in a right pickle."

The pigeon cooed, as if he understood.

"Frazzle!" Twitch hissed, having an idea. Slipping off his rucksack, and unzipping the front pocket, he pulled out a silver message capsule. "Frazzle, you're my only hope," he whispered, tearing a strip of paper from a blank page at the back of his field journal. "I need you to take a message…" He paused, remembering his mum was out. Maybe Ava would explore the house and find the pigeons. He had to try; he didn't know what else to do. He dug out a pen and wrote:

HELP! URGENT MESSAGE FOR JACK!
I'm up the hide tree without a pigeon.
Loot wars are go! Danger in the
hide! Twitch

Rolling the note into a tight scroll, he tucked it into the silver capsule and screwed on the lid. Opening the cage, he took hold of Frazzle and strapped the capsule to his leg.

"I need you to be a hero, Frazzle. I need you to give this message to a human, OK? Any human will do, but preferably Jack, or Mum, or Amita."

Frazzle stared back at him, unblinking.

"Good luck," Twitch whispered. He kissed the top of the bird's head and launched Frazzle into the air. The pigeon flapped his wings, landed on a branch just above Twitch's head, and promptly dropped back down to the platform and waddled up to Twitch and pecked at the pallet, looking for more seed.

"No, go home. *Shoo!*"

Frazzle hopped away, offended, flapped into the air and landed in the opposite tree, looking back at Twitch.

"Crrrrrrrrrooooooo."

Twitch rubbed his hands over his face, wishing he'd brought Squeaker instead of Frazzle, but when he looked back up, the pigeon was gone.

26
NIGHT OWL

Moonlight reflecting off the surface of the pond lit up the nightly dance of insects above the still water. Twitch clenched his teeth to stop them from chattering. It was lonely up the tree without Frazzle. He was worried about his pigeon and beginning to wish he hadn't released him. Frazzle had never flown in the dark. There was a good chance he'd get lost or, worse, picked off by a nocturnal predator. He pushed together the poppers of his shirt, doing it right up, and unrolled the sleeves. He tried to ignore how cold his legs were. All he could do was sit and wait.

He heard the call of a tawny owl. Lifting his binoculars, he slowly turned his head, searching for the solitary hoot-maker. He hadn't seen a tawny owl since his grandad was alive.

"Hoo hoo-hoooo hooo-o-o…"

Twitch let his ears lead his head. He caught the reflection of the moon in two disc-like eyes. The owl's body was so well camouflaged he couldn't see where the tree ended and the bird began. He focused his binoculars and waited.

The owl's head jerked. Its eyes locked on to something. The wings rose, coming together, back to back, almost vertically, above its head, and they pushed the Earth away as the owl emerged into the night sky like a deadly vigilante.

Twitch felt his soul rise with it. He couldn't just sit here, waiting to be rescued. He needed to do something, fight back. He wanted to help Tippi and Ava, and Gwen Ryan. Billy, or Fergal, or whatever his name was, couldn't be allowed to get away with destroying people's lives like this. It was easier, he realized, to think of the man as Fergal, because he'd liked Billy. But Billy had never really existed.

Twitch wished he had a flare gun that would attract the attention of the police – if they discovered Fergal Doherty was alive, they'd know Gwen Ryan didn't kill him. But Ava had already pointed out that it wouldn't prove her mum had nothing to do with the robbery. He needed to find a way to get Fergal to confess.

"Pssstttt!"

Twitch almost jumped out of his skin. His head snapped round at the unnatural sound, and his heart drummed a paradiddle. To his astonishment and joy he saw Jack straddling the branch of an adjacent tree, working his way closer to him until the bough began to bend under his weight.

Twitch crawled to the edge of the platform. Slithering on his stomach, he pulled himself along the closest of the three sturdy branches, stretching out as far as he could, clinging to it with knees and thighs until his head was two metres from Jack's. He signalled that they had to be quiet.

Jack nodded and pointed down.

Twitch saw Ava, Tippi, Ozuru and Terry standing at the foot of Jack's tree, waving up at him. Amazed, Twitch wondered if Frazzle had somehow found Jack. Or maybe the girls had brought him. It didn't matter. He was so glad Jack was here. His desire to serve Fergal Doherty a slice of justice flamed brighter. Together he was certain they could do it.

Jack started moving his hands and Twitch realized he was trying to communicate using sign language, but he was fast and it was dark, and Twitch only knew the alphabet.

"Listen," Twitch mouthed, barely making a whisper.

"I have to apologise to you. Billy lied to us both, and I thought... I thought..."

Jack was shaking his head. "We're quits," he replied, and smiled. "But what are we going to do?" He pointed at the hide.

"I've got a plan. Everyone" – Twitch circled his hand over them all – "go to my neighbour's house. Amita's." He paused and Jack nodded.

"I'm going to lead Billy to my house. Pretend the loot is there."

Jack frowned and shook his head, whispering, "Too dangerous."

"It's the only way."

"Then what?"

"Rescue me." Twitch grinned at Jack. "I trust you."

Jack studied Twitch, then gave him a thumbs up and started to work his way backwards along his branch.

By the time Twitch was back on his platform, Jack was on the ground and whispering animatedly in a huddle with the others. Ozuru and Terry ran off together towards the footpath. Twitch wondered where Jack had sent them, or perhaps they had got cold feet and run home. Expecting Jack, Ava and Tippi to disappear off to Amita's at any second, Twitch prepared himself to face Fergal. His plan was to make a loud noise and get caught, then let it slip that he was in league with the Kingfisher girls and that they and the stolen money were back at his house. Then it would be up to Jack to rescue him.

Having a plan seemed to have heated his body. He had stopped shivering. Pulling on his rucksack, he carefully climbed down to the hatch in the hide roof, steeling himself for the anger of Fergal Doherty.

"Hey, Twitch, you in there?"

Twitch felt a physical shock at Jack calling his name. What was he playing at? He climbed back up the tree so he could see what was going on. Fergal had come out of the hide and was standing opposite Jack.

"Oh, hey, Billy. I'm looking for Twitch. Have you seen him?" Jack sounded casual and relaxed, as if this were the most normal situation in the world. "He's been kicking about all day with those girls from the canal boat and avoiding me."

"You've seen him with the Kingfisher girls today?"

"Yeah, earlier this afternoon. He was taking them and their nan to his house. He said their boat had flooded. They had big bags with their stuff in."

"Why, the lying little…" Fergal hissed to himself.

"What are you doing out here, in the hide?" Jack asked. "You watching birds?"

"You could say that." Fergal's voice had a dangerous undertone. "Listen, Jack. I borrowed Twitch's binoculars to watch the birds, but now I realize I don't know how to get them back to him. I don't know his address."

"I can give them to him tomorrow, if you want. I know where he lives."

"Do you?" Fergal advanced a step towards him and Jack shuffled back. "Because I'd like to go and see him *right now*." He grabbed Jack by the scruff of his T-shirt. "Let's go."

Twitch watched Fergal march away, dragging a frightened-looking Jack alongside him. He was numb with shock. What was Jack doing? This wasn't the plan!

Clambering down the tree, he opened the hatch and dropped into the hide. Gwen was still sat on the ground, but now Ava and Tippi were either side of her, Ava untying her hands, Tippi showering her with kisses. He couldn't help staring at her cheek, which was swollen and bruised.

"Are you OK?" he asked, wondering if it was his fault that Fergal had hurt her.

"I'm fine." She nodded, and as if she could read his mind added, "I wound Fergal up about the money until he lost his temper." She smiled. "That was a neat trick, by the way, climbing up the tree. You were silent as a cat."

"Ava, what is Jack doing?" Twitch said, kneeling to help untie Gwen's ankles.

"He said that you had a plan, and that he was going to lead Fergal to your house. He sent Ozuru and Terry to gather reinforcements and told them to get as many kids as they could to go to your next-door neighbour's house and bring weapons."

"But that's not the plan. The plan was that *I* was going to lead Fergal to my house."

"Yes, he said that was your idea. He also said that you trusted him, and he thought you'd be much better at rescuing him than he would be at rescuing you. So he changed the plan."

"But Fergal might hurt him!"

"Fergal might have hurt you," Ava pointed out.

"What are we going to do now, Twitch?" Tippi asked.

"We're going to rescue Jack," Twitch replied. He looked at Ava, Tippi and Gwen Ryan. "We're going to capture Fergal and get him to confess. Then we'll turn him over to the police and clear your mum's name."

27

THE PEACOCK ROOM

"What's that noise?" Ava stood up. She looked at her mum in alarm. "I can hear dogs barking."

Twitch turned off the lantern and they stared at each other in the dark.

"Police sniffer dogs," Gwen Ryan said, coming on to all fours. "I have to get into the water, quick, or the dogs will smell me and they'll catch me." They leaped out of her way as she crawled from the hide, running towards the water. There was yelling and barking; floodlights raced over the ground, meeting to light her up. They heard pounding feet and the shouting of orders. Suddenly the edge of the pond was swarming with police.

"Mum!" Ava gasped, as several officers went wading into the water after her.

Twitch closed the hide door and opened the

window. The three of them huddled in front of it, watching with horror as Gwen Ryan was dragged out of the pond and handcuffed. Three dogs, pulling an officer, came sniffing around the hide, but they were yanked away and shouted at for chasing rabbits.

"What do we do?" Ava whispered. She had her arms around Tippi, who'd buried her face in her sister's chest and was whimpering.

"Same as before," Twitch said with gritted teeth. "We're going to rescue Jack, capture Fergal, turn him in and clear your mum's name. This all ends tonight."

Ava nodded, a steely expression on her face. "We won't get any help from the police. They're all out there arresting my mother. They think they've already got the bad guy."

"If my idea works, we won't need the police."

They heard the sound of a helicopter.

"How are we going to get out of here?" Ava asked.

"Stick close to me. I know a way through the trees that avoids the main paths," Twitch ordered. "If we get stopped, we'll say we're just curious to see if Robber Ryan has been caught. We'll head straight to Amita's house, keeping our eyes peeled for Jack and Fergal. Hopefully Ozuru and Terry will be able to drum up some help."

"Tippi, did you hear that?" said Ava softly to her sister. "I need you to be brave now, for me and for Mummy. Twitch has got a plan. OK?"

Tippi wiped her eyes and screwed up her face. "I'm going to punch Fergal and kick him in the nuts."

"That's my girl," Ava said, looking at Twitch. "We're ready."

They followed Twitch out of the hide, sidling round to the rabbit trail and ducking into the cover of the trees. They moved swiftly and Twitch kept up a steady pace, choosing his paths with care, refusing to let fear make them run in case they tripped or had an accident. They hid once, when officers passed them on the way to the pond.

"Did you hear? They've caught her," one said.

"About time," another grumbled.

Twitch glanced at Ava, but her face was unreadable. He thought about Jack, and hoped Fergal wouldn't lose his temper when he reached Twitch's house and discovered the girls and the money weren't there.

They sped back along the towpath and through the streets towards Twitch's house. He gave Tippi a piggyback some of the way when she got tired. They crept up Sunningdale Street, their eyes fixed on the end house. The lights were off. They arrived at number 53 breathless, their pulses racing, and tapped quietly on Amita's door.

It opened immediately. On seeing Twitch, Amita opened her mouth to speak, but he put a finger to his lips and hurried in, making her wait until they were inside and the door was closed.

"What in goodness is going on?" Amita asked.

"I can explain," Twitch said. "Amita, I need your help. My friends Ava and Tippi" – he pointed at them by way of introduction – "need your help too. This is a very serious situation."

"You are telling me this is a very serious situation. Take a look at this..."

She pushed open the door to her living room, which Twitch had always called the peacock room because Indian peafowl featured heavily in the patterns on the turquoise walls, in the gold-stencilled midnight-blue ceiling and in the mosaic beneath the glass coffee table. Peacocks were even embroidered on the clashing cushions, and carved onto the ornaments, candlesticks and lamp stands. His jaw dropped as he saw the room was jammed full of kids from his year at school; some he'd never even spoken to. He scanned the faces. Three boys from science class were sat on the floor trading football cards. Two girls he didn't know the names of were looking about wearing bored expressions.

"Did you tell people you were having a party at my house?" Amita asked.

"No!" Twitch replied, his heart hiccupping as he saw that Tara was here, standing beside Sybil, a girl from his form. Ozuru was sat awkwardly on the sofa beaming at him and holding a fishing rod. There was a knock at the front door behind him, and in trooped Terry, followed by Vernon and the star of the school football team, Clem Buckskin.

"The muscles have arrived," Vernon announced, flexing his biceps as they joined everyone in the peacock room. He looked at Twitch and said eagerly, "Terry says we can punch someone."

There was another knock and Twitch was surprised to see Amita showing Pamela Hardacre in. She scowled at him.

"I think that's everyone," Terry said to Twitch.

"How did you get them all to come?" Twitch was amazed.

"Just sent a message round." Terry held up his phone, smiled and sat down next to Ozuru. "We're ready."

They all stopped their whispered conversations and turned to look at Twitch.

It was blinding, the attention of so many kids from his year. He could tell a few of them had no idea who he was. He tried to swallow but his mouth felt like it was full of feathers. Amita tapped him on the shoulder. She'd put an upside-down crate on the floor beside him, indicating he should stand on it. He steeled himself, tucking his fringe behind his ear so they could all see his face and stepped up. "Thank you for coming. For those of you who don't know me, my name's Twitch." Someone sniggered. "You were asked to come here because next door there is a hostage situation." That got their attention. "A man called Fergal Doherty has kidnapped Jack Cappleman and is holding him captive." There were gasps. "Fergal is a dangerous criminal; he's extremely strong and known to be violent."

"I shall call the police immediately!" Amita exclaimed.

"The police are all at Aves Wood," Twitch replied, "where they've arrested Gwen Ryan."

"Robber Ryan's been caught?" Tara asked.

"Robber Ryan's a *girl*!" Vernon looked at Clem, who appeared equally confused.

"Girls rob banks too, you know," Pamela said, looking down her nose at them.

"Don't say that!" Tippi shouted, shocking them into silence. "She's my mum."

Ava stepped forward. "Gwen Ryan is no robber. The man she's supposed to have murdered is Fergal Doherty. But he's not dead; he's next door. He faked his own death and he framed our mum for armed robbery."

There were more gasps then excited whispering.

"The police are busy. They won't get here quickly and they may not even believe us," Twitch said, "so we need to save Jack before he gets hurt." He paused. "None of you have to help us. You didn't know what you were signing up for when you came here, so if you want to leave, I understand." He looked around the room at the focused faces and a fully formed idea hatched in his head. "But I do have a plan to rescue Jack, capture Fergal and clear Gwen Ryan's name, and I'd *really* like you to help me."

"I'm in," Vernon said, punching his fist into his hand, and there were mutters of agreement and heads nodding all around the room.

"Right then, listen up," Twitch said, "because this is going to sound really weird."

28

BIRDBRAIN

Amita brought Twitch a large piece of paper. He laid it on the mosaic table in the middle of the peacock room and sketched a plan of the ground floor of his house. Everyone gathered in a circle around him.

"There are no lights visible from the front of my house, which means Jack and Fergal must be in the kitchen." He drew a large cross. "When you come through the front door, you run straight down the hall and you're in the kitchen. The living room is to your left; ignore that door and the one next to it. The only really dangerous weapons in the kitchen are the knives. They are kept in a knife block here." He marked the map. "Fergal must not be allowed up this end of the kitchen. If he gets hold of a weapon, we're in trouble."

Pamela raised her hand. "Um, I don't want to put a dampener on this Secret Seven tribute party, but how on earth are we" – she circled her hand – "going to take down an angry armed robber?" She looked at everyone with a pitying expression. "We're hardly a pack of Tyson Furys, more like a bunch of fluffy kittens and mega nerds." She flicked back her long blonde hair and looked pointedly at Twitch.

"Hey! I like fighting," Vernon protested.

"Firstly, Fergal's not armed," Twitch said, raising his hands to get the group to focus on him. "Secondly, we're going to play to our strengths. Terry and Ozuru told you to bring weapons?" Heads nodded. "Great, show me what you've got."

"I brought my hockey stick." Sybil held it like a staff.

"I brought my American football helmet and my boxing gloves," Vernon said proudly.

"I brought my older brother's cricket pads," Tara said, pointing to a carrier bag at her feet, "and his bat."

"I brought my skateboard," Clem said.

Twitch raised an eyebrow but nodded, moving on to Terry.

"I couldn't think of anything," Terry confessed. "I guessed we might need to tie him up, right? So I went into my garage to look for rope. Turns out we don't have any rope, but I did find a box with reels of gaffer tape in it. So I brought that."

"You couldn't have grabbed a hammer?" Pamela said, looking unimpressed.

"I don't want to hit anyone with a hammer." Terry winced. "I don't like blood."

"I'm not good at fighting," Ozuru admitted. "So I brought my fishing rod, this" – he waved a red rectangular box with brightly coloured buttons – "and a loudhailer."

"What's that do?" Pamela pointed at the box. "Because if it doesn't let out a deadly sleeping gas…"

Ozuru pressed a button and it made a fart noise.

Pamela laughed. "Wow, are we in trouble!"

"It makes other noises," Ozuru protested, pressing another button and the *dooiiinnnggg!* of a spring sounded from the red box.

"What did you bring, Pamela?" Twitch asked.

"I brought myself and my phone," she replied, holding it up with a challenging look on her face, "because that is all I need to bring down an armed robber."

"Great." A knot of anxiety twisted Twitch's stomach.

"Ava and I don't have anything," Tippi said apologetically.

"I have a frying pan," Amita said from the doorway, brandishing her weapon. "And a catapult if someone wants to borrow it?"

Twitch tried to smile confidently at everyone, whilst simultaneously wondering if a bunch of kids and an old lady with bric-a-brac weapons would be enough to bring down Fergal Doherty. He knew the man would have no qualms about hurting any of them. Twitch was scared, but he wasn't about to let Jack down. He took a deep breath. "OK, this is what we're going to do."

Everyone leaned closer.

"We're going to pretend we are starlings."

There was an immediate clamour of objections.

"Are you talking about birds?" Terry sat back in disgust. "Now?"

"Is something wrong with you?" Vernon asked.

Pamela was shaking her head. "Birdbrain."

"We're doomed," Ozuru declared.

"Listen to me!" Twitch shouted, losing his patience. "Starlings are small birds; they are easy for a large predator to kill. Fergal Doherty is a large predator. He is a falcon, an eagle or a hawk. We are small birds. We are starlings."

The room simmered down to silence.

"Starlings do this amazing thing to protect themselves from predators. It's called a murmuration."

"A what now?" Pamela cocked her head.

"A murmuration." Twitch lifted a hand to stop

her from interrupting again. "They gather in large numbers, in flocks of thousands, and do this amazing dance, at dusk. They fly as a group, wheeling and turning constantly, undulating and moving like a three-dimensional mathematical pattern. Why? Because there's safety and power in numbers. Many starlings are capable of overwhelming one predator. But that's not all. The dance is confusing. It makes it hard for a predator to focus on picking off one bird. It's an incredible thing to see. It's like the ultimate in group togetherness."

"And you want us to … murmurate?" Tara asked hesitantly.

Twitch nodded. "Yes."

"Somebody kill me now," Pamela muttered.

"People who study murmurations have noticed that each bird is aware of the seven birds immediately around it and makes split decisions about its own movement based on those seven birds. There are twenty-two of us, twenty-one if you take away Ava."

Ava frowned. "Why would you take me away?"

"There's something else I need you to do. I'll tell you in a minute."

Ava clamped her mouth shut, obviously not happy with this part of the plan.

"We will divide into three squadrons of seven to enter the house. Vernon, you're leader of the first squadron." He pointed to Ozuru, Clem and four others. "You're all squadron one. Tara, you lead squadron two." Pamela winced as he pointed at her, Sybil and the boys from science class. "You're with Tara. Then there's me, Terry, Amita, Tippi, you, you and you. We're squadron three." He hoped they hadn't realized he didn't know their names.

Everyone immediately started discussing which group they'd been put in. Twitch stepped up onto the crate and they all fell silent.

"Fergal's got Jack." He felt a thrill to see they were really listening to him now. "He's hurt our friends. Now he's going to get what he deserves."

There were approving murmurs.

"Here are the rules of the murmuration formation. Everyone has to keep moving *all the time*. You are not allowed to stand still for a second. If you do that, it gives Fergal an opportunity to hit you. We can't let that happen. Think … the floor is lava. You must always be aware of where everyone is and what they're doing. Move towards each other; but don't crowd one another. We have to move as one. Play to your strengths. You know what you are good at; do that. If one of us shouts, we all must listen. Once we are in the kitchen, in the murmuration formation, there are no leaders any more; we are all leaders."

Everyone was looking at each other and nodding. Twitch could feel the group drawing together and getting stronger.

"On our own, we're not strong, but together, *together*, we're a force to be reckoned with."

"Yeah!" Vernon cheered. "Let's murmurate!"

29
MURMURATION FORMATION

"That was a commanding speech you gave down there," Amita said to Twitch as they climbed the stairs to her bathroom. "Iris would be proud." She paused. "I don't suppose you know when your mother is coming home?"

Twitch shook his head. "Let's hope it's not till really late." He clambered out of Amita's bathroom window and dropped silently onto the flat roof above his kitchen. It was completely dark now.

"Terry, you next," Twitch whispered. "Careful not to land heavily or Fergal will hear."

Terry wriggled out of the window with his carrier bag and stood beside Twitch.

"Now, Tippi." Twitch reached up to help her, but she was as light and graceful as a gymnast and needed no help.

Amita's bottom loomed as she shuffled backwards through the window and Twitch crossed arms and linked hands with Terry to make a seat for her to sit into. They lowered her noiselessly to stand beside them. She was clutching her frying pan and her eyes were twinkling. He'd never seen her look so excited.

"Don't make a sound," Twitch whispered to the others who followed after.

They crept to the edge of the roof in single file. Twitch pointed to the water butt that collected rain from the gutters. He indicated that Terry should climb onto it, then to the ground. Terry scrambled down easily. Tippi followed, and Twitch held Amita's frying pan while she descended. When all six of them were on the ground looking up at him, he gave them a thumbs up.

"You know what to do," he whispered and they nodded. "Right, I'm going in."

"Good luck," Amita hissed, and Twitch saw Terry cross his fingers.

As he crept to the pigeon loft, Twitch tucked his camo shirt into his trousers, pulling it out a bit so it ballooned over his belt. He loaded the pockets of his combats with birdseed, then opened the wardrobe door.

"Frazzle! You made it home!" He'd never felt so

pleased to see a bird. He looked at the pigeon's leg and saw that the silver capsule wasn't there. He didn't have time to solve that mystery. He picked up the bird and carefully lowered him into the space between his tee and camo shirt. Then he did the same with Scabby, Maude and Squeaker. There was some cooing and scratching of claws, but the birds didn't seem to mind the dark warm space.

Walking very carefully, with arms wrapped protectively around his bird belly, he climbed into his bathroom through the open window and crept down the stairs. Hugging the wall, Twitch sidled along to the front door and opened it, pulling down the catch to keep it on the latch. Outside, the murmuration formation was armed and waiting. He nodded at them, then tiptoed along the hall towards the kitchen, sinking one hand into his pocket and grabbing a load of seed.

Fergal was standing with his back to the door and his hands on his hips. Jack was tied to a chair, facing him. Twitch could see that one of his eyes was swollen and there was a trickle of blood coming from his nose. A surge of fury exploded in his chest; he threw back his head and gave a piercing whistle as he ripped open his shirt and flung the birdseed at Fergal.

"What the—?" Fergal spun round as the four pigeons flew at him, confused and excited by the food. He cried out, lifting his arms to bat the birds away. Twitch zigzagged across the room, grabbing Jack's chair and dragging it backwards out of the murmuration zone.

Outside, underneath the kitchen window, Tippi held Ozuru's loudhailer and sound box. When she heard Twitch's whistle, she hit the button that played a police siren and directed the speaker into the loudhailer.

Fergal cried out again, spinning round to face the window as a stream of howling children galloped into the kitchen behind him. A barrage of eggs, shot by a catapult through the open back door, hit Billy in the face.

Twitch dropped to his knees, working at the knots that held Jack to the chair.

"Go on!" Jack cheered. *"GET HIM!"*

Vernon, dressed in helmet and boxing gloves, charged head first like a bull at Fergal's stomach. Taken by surprise, Fergal stumbled, and Vernon managed to strike a few body blows before he was knocked aside.

Fergal launched himself towards the knife block, trying to grab himself a weapon, but Tara was there in her cricket pads with her bat, and she whacked his hand, crushing it against the worktop.

Fergal yelled angrily.

Pamela, who was standing in the kitchen doorway, started screaming as if she were being murdered, and pointed her phone at him.

Fergal, turning his head at the noise, became alarmed when he saw the phone and lurched towards her, but she pirouetted away into the room, following Twitch's orders not to stand still. Amita danced into the kitchen and walloped Fergal across the shoulder with her frying pan. The pigeons were still flying around the kitchen, landing briefly to grab a bit of seed then taking off again.

Ozuru, who was wailing like a banshee as he ran around, threw himself at one of Fergal's legs and clung on tightly. Terry, seeing him do this, let out a yell and launched himself through the back door at the other leg. Their eyes met and Terry, hugging Fergal's knee to his chest, pulled out the end of the gaffer tape, stuck it to the man's jeans and passed the roll to Ozuru, who pulled it round the back of Fergal's legs and returned it to Terry, who looped it round and passed it back to Ozuru.

Seeing what they were doing, Sybil, who had opted

for a jump and slide movement, whacked her hockey stick into the back of Fergal's knees. He grunted in pain, his arms flailing as he tumbled like a felled tree to the floor.

The boys from science class herded Fandango, Eggbum and Dodo into the kitchen, who clucked and squawked like crazy.

"HELL'S TEETH!" Fergal roared, lashing out with his fists trying to punch Ozuru and Terry, but Clem, who'd been hopping about trying to find his moment, knee-dropped onto Fergal's stomach holding his skateboard in front of them like a shield.

"Oooooffffff!" Fergal wheezed in pain as his fists collided with the skateboard and he felt the impact of Clem's knees.

Vernon was now back on his feet and tagged in. Clem got up and Vernon sat down on Fergal's chest, pinning his arms to the floor with his knees and holding his boxing gloves in a defensive position in front of his face.

Jack, finally free, leaped to his feet and grabbed the orange water pistol, aiming it at Fergal and squirting him in the eyes as the others gathered around him, brandishing their weapons.

Scabby flew across the kitchen to Twitch, dropping

a splatter of white poop on Fergal's forehead before landing on Twitch's shoulder.

"You did it!" Tippi cried from the back doorstep, a broad grin on her face. "You got him."

30

HOME TO ROOST

Fergal let out a stream of bad language and Terry slapped a piece of gaffer tape over his mouth.

There was a noise behind them, and they all turned to see Ava and Nan coming down the hall dragging five black duffel bags.

"Is that the stolen money?" Twitch asked.

They both nodded, staring at Fergal with wide eyes.

"Where was it hidden?" Jack asked.

"In the engine room of the *Kingfisher,*" Twitch replied.

Hearing this, Fergal writhed angrily on the floor like a furious gaffer-taped caterpillar.

Twitch opened one of the bags and pulled out a stack of cash. He ripped the tape away from Fergal's mouth. "How does it feel, Fergal, to see it but not be able to touch it?" Twitch waved the money in front of his face.

"That's *my* money!" Fergal shouted.

"Really?" Twitch shook his head. "Don't you mean it's the bank's money?"

"Listen, you little pipsqueak. Banks don't need money; they have insurance. I planned that robbery for months. It was the greatest heist since the Great Train Robbery. I executed the plan faultlessly, and it would have been perfect if it hadn't been for that bloody woman coming home from work when she did."

"But Gwen Ryan didn't know you were robbing a bank," Twitch pointed out. "It's not her fault."

"She didn't have to take the money out of the boot of the car and hide it though, did she?" Fergal snarled. "Do you know how hard it is to fake your own death?"

"No," Twitch said. "And I don't care, either." He slapped the tape back over Fergal's mouth and looked at Pamela. "Did you get it?"

"Best documentary ever!" Pamela pronounced. "And … yup … now it's uploaded to the Internet for all the world to see." She smiled innocently at Fergal. "Guess people are going to realize you're not dead pretty soon, huh?" She put a finger to her lips as if a thought was only just occurring to her. "Oh dear, I do hope the other members of your nasty robber gang don't hold a grudge. They might get a bit angry when they find out that you double-crossed them, faking your own death to steal their share of the stolen money. I'm sure you can explain it to them when you see them *in prison*."

Twitch became aware that Tara was at his side.

"Your plan was brilliant, Twitch," she said, smiling sweetly, and his tummy flipped.

Ava was beside Jack, examining his bruised face. "You're hurt."

"I'm all right," Jack said. "It only stings a bit."

"That was a very brave thing you did," Ava said sincerely. "I won't forget it."

"Hey, Jack," Twitch said. "How did you know I was up the tree?"

Jack grinned. "I found Frazzle on the towpath being bullied by crows. I chased them away and, after he'd given me the runaround, I managed to pick him up and read your message." He put his hand in his pocket and pulled out the silver capsule. "I was on my way to Aves Wood with Ozuru and Terry when we bumped into Ava and Tippi."

Amita was talking to Nan and trying to tell her the names of all the children, but she kept getting confused.

"OK, listen up, everybody." Pamela held up her

hand. "If we're going to do this right, you need to do what I say now. We are in my area of expertise." She smiled and tossed her hair. "Boys," she ordered, looking at Vernon and fluttering her eyelashes, "can you sit him up?" She pointed to Fergal. "Strap him to the chair or something." She turned to Tara and Sybil. "Girls, arrange the swag bags around him. Open them so everyone can see the loot. Take a few bundles of notes and scatter them." She waggled her fingers. "Everyone is going to stand behind the captured criminal, holding their weapons and looking victorious."

Pamela turned to Ava and Tippi, who had Eggbum in her arms. "You're the victims; you should be in the foreground giving the camera justice vibes. OK? Everyone got that?" She clapped twice and they all started moving.

"Shouldn't someone be calling the police?" Nan said to Amita as they were hustled into position behind Fergal.

"They were so busy arresting your daughter-in-law, we didn't think they'd come. So Pamela had the brilliant idea of offering an Internet news broadcaster a live video of us apprehending the robber. The children tell me this will make the police come very quickly."

Vernon ogled the bags of banknotes, helping

enthusiastically with the scattering and general flinging of money in the air. Pamela was taking the composition of the photo very seriously, positioning everyone perfectly.

"Amita, hold up the frying pan, please, that's it. Twitch, do you think we could get a pigeon on the criminal's head?"

Twitch reached into his pocket and poured birdseed on Fergal's head. Frazzle and Squeaker immediately landed and began eating.

"Perfect," Pamela proclaimed, angling her phone so that her face was in the picture too. "On three, everyone say … *murmuration!*"

She took several pictures, picked the best and checked the text she was writing with Ava. "How's this? *Gwen Ryan is INNOCENT! The real robber is Fergal Doherty, who is ALIVE and caught here with his stolen loot. #FreeGwenRyan #JusticeForGwenRyan*"

"That's perfect." Ava smiled, gratefully.

"And … done!" Pamela announced, staring at her phone. "Done … and done!" She looked up. "Pretty sure that'll go viral. I tagged in a load of journalists and news channels. Plus that picture is dynamite, if I do say so myself."

They heard the sound of approaching police sirens and fell silent. Tyres screeched. Car doors clicked open and slammed closed, then Constable Greenwood, followed by five officers, burst into the house running down the hall.

"Hello, Constable Greenwood," Twitch said. "We've caught the robber Fergal Doherty for you, with all of his stolen money." He gestured grandly with his hand, and all the others did the same.

The six police officers stared at Fergal and the children in astonishment.

Pamela took a photo.

"Don't worry." Amita leaned forward. "They were supervised by a responsible adult the whole time."

Constable Greenwood opened his mouth to speak but no words came out.

"Shouldn't you be putting handcuffs on that bad man?" Amita prompted.

"Cuff him, and get him in the car," Greenwood barked at two officers, then he turned to another two. "Bag up the money."

"Mr Doherty is a very wicked man," Amita said to the constable. She held up her hand and counted on her fingers. "He has committed a terrible robbery, perverted the course of justice by faking his own death, ruined the lives of Gwen Ryan and her daughters" – she shook her head and tutted – "and, in the last twenty-four hours, he has physically assaulted two children, Corvus Featherstone" – she pointed at Twitch – "and Jack Cappleman." She pointed at Jack. "Make sure you take their statements, because we will be pressing charges. Thank you."

Constable Greenwood looked stunned. "Thank you, er, Ms, er..."

"Mrs Inglenook. I live next door."

Twitch watched as they marched Fergal Doherty away down the hall. He saw a taxi pull up outside, and his mother got out. She stared in horror at the police cars and the man wrapped in gaffer tape being dragged out of her house.

"Twitch?" she called in alarm, hurrying inside. "Twitch, are you all right?"

"I'm here." Twitch waved at her. "I'm fine. Don't worry."

Iris Featherstone's face collapsed with relief as she grabbed her son and hugged him. She looked around her crowded kitchen, her bemused gaze coming to rest on Constable Greenwood.

"Don't worry," Amita said. "I was babysitting. He was safe the entire time."

"Twitch, what *is* going on?" Iris asked him. "Who are all these people?"

"We're Twitch's friends," Jack replied, and everybody nodded and murmured in agreement.

Twitch grinned. "You did say I could have friends over."

THE TWITCHERS

It was a strange sensation, walking through the school gates. Everything was the same, and yet everything had changed. Twitch was in year eight now, but it was the same green uniform, the same concrete buildings, and he was in the same form, with the same teacher. He wondered how this year was going to go.

When he arrived at his classroom, he stood in the doorway. Jack was sat on a desk, his feet on a chair, his hands in the air as he told some story, everyone gathered around listening. Seeing him, Jack waved Twitch over.

Twitch hesitated, feeling a ripple of apprehension, wondering if the rules of school would break down the friendship they'd built over the summer. In his head, Fergal's voice whispered, "... *what happens when you go back to school? Will Jack be your friend then?*"

"Twitch, come here," Jack called impatiently. "I've been waiting for you." He looked at the others. "Twitch and I have got something to tell you."

Twitch went and stood awkwardly by Jack's desk.

"We are starting a birdwatching club. We're going to watch the autumn migration. Who wants in?"

Ozuru raised his hand. "I watch the birds when I'm fishing with my dad. I'd like to know more about them."

"We will, of course, be solving any crimes we discover," Jack added, "because…"

"Ornithologists make good detectives," Twitch said, finishing his sentence, and they grinned at each other.

"Birdwatching detectives?" Terry nodded. "I'm in. Catching that bank robber was the coolest thing I've ever done."

"And we're expanding our pigeon-messaging system. I've got my own loft now," Jack told them proudly. "Got my first pair of birds a couple of weeks ago."

"Oh, I'd like pet pigeons," Ozuru said, looking at Twitch. "Would you teach me how to look after them?"

"Do we need any special equipment to be in this club?" Tara asked.

"Just binoculars and a notebook," Twitch replied. "A good camera is nice, but it's not essential." He thought about the beautiful camera with long zoom lens that he'd bought with his share of the reward money that they had all received for reuniting the bank with its stolen cash.

"Does your little club have a name?" Pamela asked, with a look on her face that told them she wouldn't be joining.

"We're called the Twitchers," Jack said.

"*Ewww!* No," Pamela muttered.

"Although we're birders, not twitchers," Twitch said. "It's just a play on my name."

"Yeah, because Twitch is the leader," Jack said. "He knows everything about birds."

"I don't know everything…"

"And the clubhouse is Twitch's hide. We've been working on it over the summer. Wait till you see it. It's so cool."

"If there's a clubhouse, I'm definitely in," Terry said.

"And there's an oath," Twitch said, "that we'll all take, to protect birds."

"Birds are for eating," Vernon said, getting up. "I'm out. But call me if there's going to be more fighting bad guys. That bit was fun."

"Don't worry, Ozuru," Twitch looked at him. "The first rule of bird club is there is no fighting in bird club."

Ozuru smiled gratefully.

"I'm not taking an oath to protect birds." Pamela shrugged. "That's dumb. Come on, Tara." She picked up her bag. "I bought some great new nail varnish at the weekend..."

Tara stayed where she was. "But I'm joining," she said.

"You're *what*?"

Tara nodded. "I want to do this."

Pamela's nose wrinkled. "Don't be a nerd!"

"Think about all the campaigning we do about climate change," Tara argued. "This is a part of that."

"Climate campaigning is cool. Birdwatching is for geeks." She looked down her nose at Tara. "I was fine with the solving a crime thing, because it got my photo in the papers and I earned so many new followers, but that doesn't mean I'm about to sit in ditches staring at birds with you guys. No way."

"But if you care about the planet, you care about the birds," Tara reasoned.

"I'm *not* going to be a birdwatcher." She closed her eyes and winced as if the thought tasted bad.

"Well, I am," Tara said.

"Fine. Be a nerd if you want to, but don't expect me to hang around with you." And she harrumphed away, sitting down in front of Vernon.

"So, five of us." Jack looked around. "Twitch, me, Terry, Ozuru and Tara."

"Seven if you count Ava and Tippi," Tara added.

"Which we do." Jack nodded emphatically, and Twitch smiled.

After Fergal Doherty had been arrested, Amita had invited Nan, Tippi and Ava to stay with her, whilst Gwen went through the process of being acquitted of all the charges against her. Over the summer, Jack and Twitch had spent a lot of time with the girls. Tippi loved Twitch's chickens, and they'd all go birdwatching together in Aves Wood, and hang out in the hide. At the end of the summer the girls had returned to their old home with their mum, but with promises that they'd be back to visit.

"So, what now?" Tara wondered.

"We swear an oath," Twitch said.

"What's the oath?" Terry asked.

Twitch raised his hand to his shoulder and drew his first two fingers together, tapping them twice against his thumb. "I do solemnly swear never to knowingly hurt a bird. I will respect my feathered friends and help them when they are in need. I will protect every bird, be it rare, endangered or common, and fight to conserve their habitats, or may crows peck out my eyes when I'm dead."

"I wrote that line," Jack said proudly.

"For I am a twitcher, now and for ever."

"What's with the weird fingers-thumb-snap thing?" Ozuru asked.

"That's our secret salute," Jack said. "It's sign language for *bird*." He raised his hand and repeated the gesture. "One of the things we will all learn is sign language, so we can communicate silently when watching birds."

"Who's going to teach us?" Ozuru asked.

"Me," Jack said, smiling. "I'm fluent."

"Cool." Ozuru nodded. He made the bird sign. "I, Ozuru, do solemnly swear…" He looked at Twitch for the next line and everyone around the circle joined in, doing the salute.

"Never to knowingly hurt a bird," Twitch prompted, and each of them repeated the oath after him.

"If this is the first ever day of the Twitchers," Terry said, "we should do something momentous."

"Already on it," Jack said, getting off the desk as their teacher marched in.

"What are we going to do?" Ozuru asked excitedly as he sat down in front of Jack.

"After school, at dusk, I'm taking you all up to Passerine Pike," Twitch said.

"That's a big hill," Terry grumbled.

"Why Passerine Pike, Twitch?" Tara asked.

"To see a real murmuration," he replied, sitting down next to Jack. "I want to show you how the starlings do it."

"Bet your way is better," Terry said as he sat beside Ozuru.

Twitch shook his head. "It isn't. Seeing a real murmuration is like standing on the bottom of an ocean of air, looking up at waves of birds breaking on an invisible shore. It washes away the world you think you know and, for that moment, you feel part of something bigger, something ancient."

AUTHOR'S NOTES AND ACKNOWLEDGEMENTS

The seed for this story was planted in 2016 at an entomology conference, when I first met the nature journalist Megan Shersby, and vet, author and TV presenter Jess French. Megan is a keen birder and she had met Jess at Birdfair – a festival for birders. They suggested I should go to the next festival, but I protested that I knew nothing about birds. They reminded me that once I had known nothing about insects. That year I met many birders and realized that they tend to be keen conservationists and insect appreciators. I followed bird lovers on social media, which sprinkled wonder and delight into my feeds, and I was impressed by the knowledge and passion of young birders, in particular Mya-Rose Craig, Dara McAnulty, Kabir Kaul and Indy Kiemel Greene, who were all an inspiration whilst I was writing this book. It was only a matter of time before I got myself a field guide and a pair of binoculars and joined the party. I would like to thank Stephen Moss for proofing my bird words, correcting my errors and offering kind words of encouragement about my new pastime. I heartily recommend his books to any keen birdwatchers.

When the idea for this book sprouted in my head, I knew it would be an adventure about friendship, the genius and beauty of birds, and the endless rewards of having a relationship with the natural world. In July 2019 I took my family on a research trip to Cromwell Bottom Nature Reserve, which is situated between Brighouse and Elland in the Calder Valley and is a wonderful place. We hired a canal boat and throughout the trip played a bird-spotting game. The rules were simple: if you spotted a bird and could identify it correctly, it would go in the book. It was there that I saw my first kingfisher. But I want this to be a universal story, so the Calder Valley has become Briddvale, and Cromwell Bottom is Aves Wood, because it doesn't matter where you live, amazing birds are everywhere.

The majority of this book was written in the 2020 lockdown, which was a difficult time for my family. I want to thank everyone at Walker Books for being patient and kind, especially Denise Johnstone-Burt, who is my editor, a kindred spirit and a friend. Huge thanks to all the Walker team, in particular Megan, Kirsten, Ben, Ed and everyone who has had a hand in creating the beautiful book you are holding, especially Paddy Donnelly, who is responsible for the wonderful cover.

I owe a debt of gratitude to my mighty agent, Kirsty McLachlan; to my writing partner, Sam Sedgman, for helping me make time to write this book; to my sister for the encouragement and the countless bird articles; to my husband, Sam, who is my partner in every possible sense of the word; and my sons, Arthur and Sebastian, for spotting the birds and making this book such a special one to write.

It is a cause of great sadness to me that my mother-in-law, Jane Sparling, to whom this book is dedicated, did not live to read it. I tend to write for a particular person. My beetle books were written for my eldest son, my train books are for my youngest son and my husband, but this book is for Jane. She believed in helping others, in kindness, in the power of having a relationship with nature; and she loved birds, especially her allotment robin. She spent her life helping the people around her, from the children who passed through her classrooms, to those she supported as a Samaritan. She helped her sons, she helped my sons and she helped me. Jane is and always will be my mother and my friend. She was such a champion of my writing for children. I love her and miss her very much.

M. G. LEONARD is an award-winning, bestselling writer of children's books, as well as a founding member of Authors4Oceans. Her books are sold in forty countries, and there is currently a TV series in development based on her Beetle Boy series. Her first picture book, *The Tale of a Toothbrush*, is out now. She is also co-author of the critically-acclaimed Adventures on Trains series. Before becoming a writer, M. G. Leonard worked as a digital media producer for the National Theatre, The Royal Opera House and Shakespeare's Globe. She lives in Brighton with her husband, two sons and pet beetles.

#TheTwitchers
@WalkerBooksUK
@MGLnrd

Enjoyed *Twitch*?
Join the Twitchers Club!

www.TwitchersClub.com
#TheTwitchers